The White Maze

Arunima

Published by "The Great Indian Book Tour"
Imprint : Holistic Publishing
www.tgibt.com
email : prashant@tgibt.com

Title : **The White Maze**
Author : **Arunima**
Copyright © Arunima 2022
All rights reserved

First published in 2022
First Edition 2022

ISBN : 978-93-93262-03-5

... to my Sister

ABOUT THE AUTHOR

Arunima comes with the world at her feet, the epistles of men in her thoughts, and the emotions of life in her words. Taught by experiences best left to the pen, brought up by adversities known yet uncommon to men, sifted by a past treasured by generations.... With quite a wealth of experience in human psychology, human management, and human anatomy, she expresses the depths of human wickedness and the heights of love, the wonders of friendship and the pain of loss, the beauty of sex and the horrors of rape, the wonder of professionalism and the dismay of blind religiosity, the peace in having a home and the dismay of its loss. Bejeweled with the stories of men telling tales to her mind, she expresses what others wouldn't. Her stories are told in the rarest of ways, caught in suspence by character and events, with the twists of reality where your neighbour truly could be the foe. After the unsurpassed success of her debut novel THE FERAL FATHER, she's engaged again with another tale of someone's past, the enigma of someone's present, and the picture of a future never to be left to chance. This Maze is a journey... join the train.

Contents

The Raging Sea	1
Emerging Life Contrasts	6
The Lord and the Lust	11
Sweet and Sour	17
First day of marriage	22
Identity Issues	27
Hidden in Shadows	32
What Makes the Man	37
Bottles of Gold	42
Assassins'	46
Women Ways	51
Staying Afloat	57
The Fight for Life	66
Duty to Self	72
Revealing the Nuts	77
In the Den	82
It was Murder	88
The Return of Reality	95
Obituaries	101
Good lives matter	110
The Bapats	115
Seeping out Truth	125
Reminiscences	131

Comrades   136

The freedom of Mortals   140

The Beginning of the Crusade   146

The Sting of Fate   154

Death is stealthy   159

Mohini   165

Love always wins   172

Keva Bai   178

The Evidence   188

Confessions   192

Time for Business   197

End to Lawlessness   201

The Army of convenience   205

A Final Twist   209

CHAPTER ONE

The Raging Sea

The sea stays blue when the sky is clear, turns black at night and takes the colour of what's beneath it in bright sunlight. The shores are the place of leisure and love, games at daylight is easily replaced by drunkenness at evening and often crazy orgies at night. The sea is not well known by divers, having seen the impossible severally; sea animals looking diabolic, treasures unprecedented, and sometimes, dead bodies of animals and humans with questionable causes. Of all these, dead human bodies are becoming more unnaturally frequent at sea.

And there is something eerie about human bodies which have been in water for any duration longer than should be. The luckier ones, once they have touched the bottom of the water body, become fodder for the Aquarian life thriving at such depths. And these don't believe in wasting their supplies. The flesh, the innards, the softer portions of the bones and the cartilage are eaten up, piece by piece. Sometimes the hair becomes a problem. The keratin in them, is quiet resilient. Tasteless and without much nutritional value, they are often omitted like teeth. The teeth get lost in the stones and pebbles and are not minded much. They have the luxury to disintegrate in their own time, neither attracting attention nor repulsion. But hair, on the hand, is a muse for sonnets and odes while it is in its correct place; but when one finds it entangled with a fish caught or worse still, comes attached to a body, it is not welcome. Separating the fish from the mangle is sometimes so difficult, that the whole catch is wasted; and not to mention the whole ordeal of informing the authorities about it. Not the fish… the hair! The once long lustrous hair, combed and braided, or rolled in a bun, or just left open after a wash to wave itself dry in the hot dry wind, adorned with flowers, lined with vermilion… once which must have enticed a lover and maybe some time made someone jealous; now coiled into impossible tangles, with none of its prior glamour or vanity, unlucky to have found itself in a fisherman's net.

And more unlucky is the body which accompanies it, still attached to the creased scalp. The face deformed by the choicest bites taken from the nose and most of the part of the tongue and right cheek. … The eyes had been spared, but the vitreous in them had seeped out due to the osmolality of the sea. The clothes had been ripped open at the arms and breast in an effort to accommodate the bloating putrefying body. The abdomen was pale and bluish against the rest of the body, a shade of white which could only be that of a dead person.

****

The unanticipated catch was dumped on the deck of the boat. The still body made a strange whooshing sound as water started to come out of the half eaten face. Whatever little fish were caught was sent back into the sea….the fisherman knew that today was going to be a very long day for him and his stand in the market would be empty. He looked at the body with fascination and repulsion, in equal portions. The bangles, which must have hung gracefully on dainty slim wrists, were now cutting through the puffed up flesh. If there were ring on the fingers, no one would know, because the larger fishes had feast on them. The anklets were still there, ridden a little away from the ankles. The nail paint was a bright red and looked quiet recent.

The fisherman imagined matching fingers on the stumps of the palms. When he had had enough of his staring at the definitely-feminine body on his deck, he dialed the police and told them about his find. They promised to be there on the shore as soon as they could come. Days like this make him hate fishing in these parts of the sea.

He had tried describing his catch as much as possible to the police …
they hate anything that brings them to the sea.

Was there anything else he could have said about the body? No,
there wasn't. Was he sure that the disfigured body was that of a woman. Looks so… yes, he was… well, at least whatever hasn't swollen out
of proportion revealed just as much.

He maneuvered the wheel to turn the boat back to shore, cutting
short his trip prematurely; the body jingling a little bit with the boat.

Something about the body caught his focus. The fisherman looked
at the body again. Was it his imagination or had the abdomen swollen
up a little more than it was some quarter-hour back?

His doubts were cleared with something more literal. A loud sickening popping sound, not very different from a long loud fart, was
followed by a foul smell which made the fisherman retch. So sickening
was the odor that it made the desensitized fisherman grab his towel
and wrap it around his face. Looking at the source, not so much to his
surprise, the bloated abdomen had deflated like a balloon, pooling its
accumulated contents under the body.

The fisherman had seen this happening with rotten fish which had
been in the water, later than they should have been. So it was not much
of a novelty for him. What frightened him was a budge in between the
woman's legs which had not been there previously. Layers of clothing
covered the blob like a shroud. The fisherman risked taking a look
by pulling aside the cloth with his toes. He wouldn't say that he was
surprised by what he saw, but he was indeed saddened. The child must
have been a few weeks shy of coming out in the world alive, but instead he was lying on the floor of the fisherman's boat, as pale as his
dead mother.

****

Ratan Macchi sat in reverence in the first row. Several others like
him had gathered in the open veranda of the house. They did not seem

to mind anything. Neither the scorching heat nor the notorious flies trying to feed on open sores and cuts could deter them. The people had assembled for four consecutive days.

The past three days had been disappointing. The Lord had declined to appear. It was known that He appeared only when the cumulative prayers and pleas of those present were loud enough to reach his ears. Therefore, with each passing day, more and more people gather to create the required decibel which would make Him know that He was needed.

Every month, in the beginning of the new moon, a sort of fair would present itself around the house. The richer vendors would snatch the most lucrative spots, nearest to the house. The lesser ones along with the newest additions would only get the worst tickets of the show. It was not a simple matter of a first come, first served arrangement. The area within 2 kilometers of the house had been duly marked with billboards and milestones. Each spot was priced indirectly proportionally to its distance from the house. Who got the money fished out as rent, was anyone's guess; although the fat gold rings and heavy chains sitting on the hairy chests of the assistants of the Lord, pointed them out as likely suspects.

In this monthly affair, the villagers sell everything from a hair pin to poultry. The occasion always started with the new moon, and ended only when the Lord had made His appearance. So, the vendors would be praying just the opposite to what the devotees were praying for as the longer the Lord took to hear their call, the more their wares get an opportunity to be taken up.

The young belles, looking at the bangles they do not want to buy would end up buying them on the next day. They came in throngs, their laughter rising in bursts on a personal joke or an observation that a certain boy was looking at their direction. These fairs also served the purpose for matchmaking grannies to go out in search of eligible probable brides and grooms.

All in all, the fair was the most important event in the small nondescript village situated just on the shore of the sea. The villagers, most of whom were fishermen, survived on their daily catch of fresh fish. Few adventurous ones, still young and ready to risk their lives, would venture out in the middle of the sea every once in a while to catch lobsters and crabs. One such trip would get them almost five days' worth of earnings.

This was when the sea was silent and mild as a nubile maiden. Sometimes she would be raging and even the bravest of them would keep away. But sometimes, she outwitted them by luring them with her nobility, and then becoming tumulus, consuming the hapless youths in her dark deep depths. It was known, that every five years, the sea would take her share of lives, in return for nourishing that of thousands. It was looked upon as a fair deal.

The deaths were mourned, for sure, because they were all young men with wives and young children, or old parents, but they did not mourn for long. Once a lamp was lit in one of the small colorful shrines, their grief ebbed out on its own. It had been almost five years now that a lamp had been newly lit at the altar. An atmosphere of uncomfortable anticipation was there in the air. They knew that any day now, the sea will come for her dues. If only, she could be satisfied with something else....

CHAPTER TWO

Emerging Life Contrasts

A small group of policemen, standing at the shores with an ambulance was not that uncommon a sight for this village. Once in a while, the sea would spit out a decaying body which would go unclaimed and get buried in an unmarked grave. A fleeting curiosity would bring the younger ones to investigate such bodies. As they grew up, these discoveries lost their novelty.

But today, a larger group than usual had gathered at a safe distance from the policemen. There were some murmurs here and there… a name mentioned. The crowd had been pulled here today by that name. It was not a name to be taken lightly. And if what they were saying was true, then it was indeed something to be seen and repeated to generations to come. It was a name which had ruled and seemed invincible… until today. It was difficult to imagine death and the name in the same sentence; the name… "Bapat"….

The police straightened and threw away the cheap locally made "biddies" they were smoking. A small dingy boat was making its way towards them. By the given description, the police knew that it was the one carrying the body. On being prompted to, the driver came out of the van disinterestedly, scratching his ear and yawning widely. He removed a stretcher from the back of the van and decided to sit on it while they waited for the boat to touch the shore; the policemen also ready to take charge of the mess they had been put into.

The sea graveyard also dug up noxious and macabre carcasses. The less fortunate ones ordered to deal with them were forced to fast for a couple of days after the discovery, because the stench refused to leave their uniforms and more than often, even their skins. A bottle of toddy and a visit to the brothel would help in getting back their appetites.

But, today, it was going to be different. The boat had hardly touched the shore, than the fisherman leaped out of the boat and released a volley of a partially digested early lunch into the sea. The policemen looked at each other and shrugged. They removed their shoes and socks and asked a boy standing nearby to take care of them. Then, laboriously they bent down and rolled their pants up to their knees and waddled in the sea to catch hold of the boat's keel.

A few enthusiastic youths did the same and ran forward to help the policemen. With collective efforts the boat was pulled all the way to the shore. The van driver, who had been idling till then, got down languidly and pushed the stretcher near the boat. The policemen climbed up the boat with the help of the boys and took a look at the boat's cargo. The driver had been looking up at them expectantly, waiting for their order to move the body. When they turned towards him shaking their head, he realized that the body couldn't be removed on the stretcher. The body, now strangely shriveled and putrefying at a much faster rate was submerged in its own fluids. They needed a body bag. And they needed their boss.

****

The Lord was standing at the window. The particular room, hidden from the view of those passing by was a vantage point for anyone who wanted to see the comings and goings, without being spotted themselves. The Lord knew that he had but few minutes, before he was obliged to go downstairs in the open and appease the chanters.

He adjusted his binoculars and focused the lenses just above the boat. All he could make from there was a clump of hair and the red and yellow of a saree. He was finding it very difficult to say with any certainty, whether the body in question was hers. Gauging the amount of decay, the Lord doubted that anybody would be able to tell who it was for sure. And yet… and yet… after being so careful, there was this name mentioned too close to him for his comfort.

This would be just the time, he reasoned, to go downstairs and meet his devotees. Not only would it dilute some of the hum the discovery of the body had created, but also help the people remember that he appeared on that particular day. Should any litigation occur, it would provide an alibi. When asked, where he was on such and such day, he would have hundreds of witnesses to prove that he had been there, right there amidst them. But he knew that she had died exactly a week ago.

He stowed away his binoculars and got busy getting in his paraphernalia. The pristine white dhoti and kurta, starched stiff as per his taste and ironed so exactly that the edges would show up at clean lines, would make a good portrait had somebody clicked a photograph of him. He removed his vest and jockeys, and exchanged them with a plain cotton boxer which would look decent and cover much of him; from the woes of having to wear a translucent cloth. A while silk scarf bordered with gold threads was adjusted over the left shoulder. A golden Rolex was clasped on the right wrist which matched the four rings already present on the fingers. A rudraksh mala was added for the final effect. The hair and the beard were brushed to a gleam. Then, adorned with a fresh necklace made of fragrant roses, and a bob of sandalwood oil behind his ears, the Lord started to descend …well-dressed servants and right-hand men on their knees …security men running awry.

✱✱✱✱✱✱✱✱✱✱✱✱

She knocked at the door when she found that it was locked from within. Five feet tall, back slightly bent by house chores …illiterate at best like most of the town dwellers. Having been married for three years without any kids, she had faced her full share of marriage woes. Love had not been fair to her and life had been difficult. But she prides herself on being softly strong, bearing any pain coming her way with as much weakness as strength.

It was not yet six in the morning and Lata was already feeling sad and defeated. Now-a-day, Gaurang Sahib, her husband, had started locking the door to his room. But she knew that it was not the door he was locking. It was her that he was locking out of his life.

The tray of tea and breakfast felt heavy in her hands. She knocked again. There was a click from the other side of the door, but Gaurang did not bother to swing it open for her. Balancing the tray on one hand, she turned the knob and went inside the room. Sahib had climbed right back into the bed, but she knew that he was awake. His phone lay on the small side table. She hesitated before sliding it aside to make room for the tray. With a small voice she let her husband know that his tea was here.

She stood for some time to see if he would at least acknowledge her presence. But he did not move. Just as she was turning to leave, the phone chimed. Immediately, Gaurang pushed aside his blanket and sat up. Lata continued to walk towards the door. She stole a look at him just as she was closing the door behind her. Not only was he awake, he was already texting back; his fingers flying over his phone's keyboard and his eyes bright and expectant, looking forward to the next message.

Lata wiped away the tears than sprang up every now and then. Why did she have to assume that there was another woman in his life? It could be just someone from work. She should be more understanding. After all, what did she, an illiterate woman, know about the nitty-gritties of the police world? Of course, it must be Tatya Bhau texting him for something important. She was being dramatic and over thinking, just as Gaurang always told her.

She poured herself the left over tea from the pan and put the leaves in a separate plastic bag. It would make good manure for her vegetables. Cheered up with the thought of growing her own vegetables, she sat on the threshold of the front door. The sky had turned a Junoesque hue of orange. The sun was about to rise. It was a new day, full of new possibilities. But Lata was not worried about the day. What she feared was the night, which came inevitably, in spite of the several lamps she lit in the evening.

The darkness of her nights was locked up in such a deep corner of her mind that no light could penetrate. It was darker than the Amavasya …darker than the depths of the deepest ocean, out of reach and impossible to contain. And yet… and yet… it was so easy to banish it, by a touch, a smile, or just a look of affection. The ache crept back in its place, clawing her soul on the way to its ascent. Then, it curled up into the place it had dug for itself and started to feed on Lata's sorrow.

She finished the cold tea and got up slowly, her body already tired having borne her heavy heart, all night long. She coaxed herself to walk into the garden. The cool dews collected on the grass, felt like a cold compress on her heart. The buds of various flowers that she had planted were already opening up. She caressed each of them, as if wishing them a good morning. Then she walked towards the back yard and checked on her pumpkin creepers and tomatoes plants. A foray of yellow promising plants had filled up the wire mesh on which the creeper had clung itself to. A small green pea shaped tomato was looking up at her.

Suddenly, her heart filled up with joy. A song, a hymn, praising God sprung up on her lips. The whole house filled up with her heavenly voice singing praises of the Creator. For a moment, Lata was so happy that she was entirely complete. She forgot about the part of her which craved for her husband's touch. With God in her, there was no place for anything else…

CHAPTER THREE

The Lord and the Lust

Ratan Macchi had started to feel dizzy. It had been almost four hours he had been sitting on his haunches at the ornate staircase which ran exactly at the center of the sitting room. He had neither had any water, nor any food. Food, he could do without. A towel, tied tightly across his stomach, kept him from growling in protest; but he needed water. In the last thirty minutes, he had stopped sweating; though the sun was shining right on his face. His chants were getting weaker as was that of the others. Except a few lesser driven ones, the others had not even shifted their position. They were sure, that today the Lord would take pity on them and show Himself.

A pitcher filled with water was standing in the corner, under the shade of the mango tree. Ratan stole several glances towards it, his dry throat bobbing up and down as he tried to swallow his own spit, but his tongue was stuck to the top of his mouth. It was considered sacrilege to even think of small worldly pleasures like a drink of a tall cool glass of water while waiting for the Lord. The sun was overbearing, and even ardent followers like Ratan were having second thoughts. But his mind wouldnt let him leave without the answers it wanted.

Ratan turned his thoughts within to find some recluse from his physical torment. He closed his eyes and immediately envisioned his mud house. A torn cloth fixed on the irregular window fluttering in the light breeze; no movement, no child, no hens… his fishing net hung on the plastic rope and on the other end hung few clothes left to dry…. a 10ft x 10ft room divided roughly into a place to cook and a place to sleep… on a low bed, lay a person. A slight weight had pulled the person in the hammock of loosely strung ropes. The covering sheets had almost covered up the person, except for a thin hand resting on the bed. Occasionally the hand would clench the pillow with all the might only to be followed by the most heart wrenching shriek he could still hear in his head.

Ratan opened his eyes. He was lying on the floor, and there was a kind face looking at him. The sun, blocked by the person's decorated head seemed like a halo around his head. Few roses touched the tip of his nose and someone was speaking kindly to him. Ratan realized that he had fainted and quickly pulled himself up. The person with the halo helped him sit up and offered him some water. Ratan gobbled the water way too quickly. The haloed person pulled back just in time as Ratan regurgitated all the water back. People were now looking at him with disgust. Even the man with the rose garland had seated himself as far as he could. His fainting had cost him his first position. Apparently, the person in white with a garland of roses around his neck was the Lord.

Ratan looked at the Lord. The ill-concealed disgust on his face faded his brilliance by several shades, for Ratan. He had been convinced that the Lord, this man, the purported reincarnation of Lord Vishnu Himself, would be the answer to his wife's suffering. Now, as he etched closer and closer to the man himself, as those in front of him touched his feet and took the flower given to them, his confidence started to mellow. Never the less, when his chance came, he aped the others who had preceded him.

While touching the Lord's feet he looked up expecting a slight hint of recognition. But there was none. He had been sure, that when the Lord will see him, he would recognize him instantly and ask about the wellbeing of his wife. The Lord selected a wilted marigold from the heap beside him and handed it to Ratan with a doleful smile, all the while looking at something far away.

Ratan took the flower and stood up to leave. His calves burnt and cramped as he walked. After sitting for such a long time, he couldn't feel his toes. He walked out of the veranda of the house with the pathetic flower in his hand. What would he say to his wife? She was so sure that the Lord would pay her a visit as soon as he heard about her pain. His mind went back to the day when he had been extremely honored to know that the Lord had paid them a visit. His wife had been exuberant, just as she always was after she came back from his "darshanam".

****

Ratan made his way towards his house, snaking through the crowd which had gathered around the shore. It must be something big, he thought, as most of the vendors had also left their shops to be audience to whatever was going on. Ratan was not interested in any circus. He kept walking towards his hut, his head bent low, burdened by the grief of not having been able to keep his promise to his wife.

He must have subconsciously disintegrated the measly flower, as he thought perhaps it would comfort her a little. He felt miserable and defeated. Yet, he decided to fake it and picked a flower from the small garden his wife had planted with her own hands. She need not feel bad about something she did not know… then gathering cheer and hope in his voice he shouted out gaily to his wife.

When he entered the room, there was stillness in the air, nothing moved; there was a peculiar calm and a sense of peace that touched him as well. For a minute, he thought his visit to the Lord had indeed eased his wife's pain. He bent towards her and tried to wake her up by shaking her think emaciated shoulders. The thin wasted hand moved like a rag doll. The beautiful multi colored bangles which she used to adore were so high up that they crossed her bony elbows all the way to her arm. The eyes were sunken and her mouth was slightly parted.

Even in death, she looked happy to see him. He sat down near his wife, who was now at peace and looked down at the flower. A smile crept on his face as his grief broke down from his eyes, as he thought how cross she would have been if she knew that he had plucked the flower from their garden. He placed the flower near her head and wept bitterly for the loss of his only companion.

****

The tea was milky and light, and the puran poli was soggy and way sweeter than he cared for. He decided that he would have some tea just outside his Thana, and ask Tatya to get some of the samosas he loved from the shop on his way to work. As he brushed his teeth and splashed some water on his face, he felt he could do without a shave today; so he ditched the razor he had picked up and instead got ready to take his bath.

The red bucket was filled up to half with likely warm water as left by Lata, his wife. The silly woman could have at least told him. Now the water was tepid and would not be enough. As such a loud reproach was already there on his tongue when Lata knocked again on his bath-room door. He was naked, but he had stopped caring about his wife looking at his body. It did nothing to her, and either way, he did not care. He opened the door and let her in.

As though on cue, she was carrying a big saucepan full of hot steaming water. She poured it in the bucket and left immediately, all the while, casting down her eyes. Gaurang slammed the door with more force than required. He hoped that his stupid wife could understand that he was annoyed at her inadequacies.

He turned on the tap and waited for the water to go down a few degrees to a comfortable temperature. Then, he poured the water all over him with a tumbler. As the water rolled over his body, he was filled up with the vision of Charu's naked body sliding over his. He imagined her red luscious lips closing on his nipple, while with her fingers, she stroked his other. He took some soap and started lath-ering his body. Charu's seductiveness stayed in his mind… her toes rolling his testicles slowly… her tongue licking the underside of his scrotum… her playfulness as she jumped out of reach, only to taunt him while rubbing her own breasts, till her nipples stood up, red and ripe, ready to be sucked.

Gaurang had a hard erection. He looked at his image in the wall mirror. He was any woman's dream. He stroked his penis which was almost touching his abdomen… so aroused was he. Then he started to stroke himself with the soapy hands; gliding his foreskin easily. All the while he looked in the mirror and marveled at his physique. He was unstoppable. He was God's best creation. He was there to rule… And with that last thought, he came. The semen poured; some of it falling in the bucket of water; the white blob disappearing in the water. He sucked his teeth and wondered what to do next. He decided to use the contaminated water, after all.

He poured the water hastily all over him, with the gayatri mantra, which he recited habitually during his baths. Maybe chanting the powerful mantra was a sacrilege… but by the time he decided to stop, he had already chanted it a couple of times, and the water had also finished. Well, it was what it was.

As he toweled his body and started to put on his uniform, which was miraculously already arranged on the bed, with a fresh pair of socks and polished shoes, he was a little worried about what had happened in the bathroom.

Sahib Gaurang was a superstitious man. He knew that his little act of self-pleasure and chanting the mantra in that condition was bound to boomerang back at him. He was sure that he was going to get some bad news. Will it be Charu, yet again refusing to meet up? Or was it going to be his superior taking him up on the third degree torture he had subjected that young thief?

He left the house on his motorcycle, still contemplating what horrendous news awaited him. He did not see Lata standing behind the gate with her hand raised in a wave…

****

The happiness ebbed away again. She dragged herself through each room, arranging stuffs and cleaning, mechanically. When she reached the bedroom, she saw the tray; the tea, cold and discolored, and the puran poli, torn from one of its edge and left uneaten. The grief of rejection was way too much for her. She flung herself on the bed and buried her face in the blanket which had covered her husband. Her body shook in silent sobs.

Once spent, she got up, her nose uncomfortably blocked, and her eyes red and swollen. She picked up the blanket and folded it. Then she straightened and dusted the bed sheet. She fluffed the pillows and arranged them neatly. After she had finished sweeping and mopping, she took the tray off the table and sat down on the bed. She rolled the thick soft Puran poli and finished all of it in two bites. The food and the sweetness soothed her jarring nerves. She picked up the empty tray and made her way out. This day shall also pass.

CHAPTER FOUR

Sweet and Sour

The music was so loud, that Mahesh could literally feel his ear drums caving in with the bass. If it was possible to hear with one's skin, then that was exactly what the groom was doing. After having faced the embarrassment of having fallen off the mare in his first attempt, his mood had been subdued. The rented suit was lined by some cheap material which was prickly and created static sounds whenever he moved his arms or legs. The trousers were uncomfortably tight and were hitching high up his groin, making him look as if he had a permanent erection.

Everything about his attire was wrong. Never in his life had he worn underwear like the one he was wearing right now; but his brother had insisted that he put it on, as he was getting married. What had underwear got to do with getting married? But his inebriated brother was beyond logic. In this tipsy condition, it was do as told. And as a clap or punch minutes before getting married did not seem like a very good idea to Mahesh, he decided to suffer silently, and go through the day with minimum drama.

His friends and many of his cousins, whom he had never seen in his life, were dancing obscenely on some salacious song. He was being carried on a mare with the owner leading the mare by a rope. The mare, was trotting along, unfazed by this demonstration of absurdity. She must have seen all of it, Mahesh thought, considering the clumps of bare pink skin peeking out from the blanket covering her back. Mahesh touched the neck of the mare and was surprised by the texture of the mane. It was rough and matted like raw unprocessed jute. He tried to take a closer look, but the owner of the horse slapped his hand away, asking him rudely, to keep his hands to himself. So, for the rest of the journey, the poor groom, strapped and wrapped in the glitter and glamour of a day, put his hands on his thighs, as he made way to the bride's house.

The lights had been arranged in such a way, that when switched on, they made the broken edges and the caved in parapet look symmetrical and pristine. A red carpet, stained with carelessly dropped food in many of the marriages, was laid out from the road, all the way to the bride's house, poorly concealing the irregular and rough ground underneath. A huge cut out of Styrofoam in the shape of two hearts merging had been decorated with the brightest colors the maker had at hand. The hot pink 'M' of the groom and the emerald green 'U' of the bride was pierced together by a golden arrow. Three men were trying to put the piece of art above the entrance. Like the rest of the people, even these men were a little drunk and so were finding this job very stressful and impossible. The fact that they were trying to put it upside down was missed by all of them. When they couldn't do it and the band could be heard just round the corner, the bride's groom pulled all the three of them away and rewarded them with sound slaps. The reprimanded men did not take it too well. So they broke the entangled hearts into two and dumped it unceremoniously at one corner.

Uma was eagerly looking forward to the wedding. All of nineteen, she was bursting with questions about 'that thing'. She had heard her friends discuss the thing in miniscule detail, and she had found herself tingle at places her mother had taught her were shameful. For a long time, she had followed the book of conduct laid out for her by her parents. Any discussion about the shameful parts or any scene showing those things were taboo for her.

Until one fateful day, when she had returned a little early from school and found her parents not only having their own shameful parts out, but were also doing unthinkable things. She had withdrawn from the house without a sound and had run down to her safe place, a hollowed cave-like place, hidden amidst the huge rocks at the sea shore. There she had mentally repeated what she had seen, as if it was on a loop.

Since then, she tore the hypothetical book and decided never to feel ashamed about her body. In the coming years, she had seen and felt her own body as well that of horny pimpled teenage boys in her class. Her name started to be taken with awe amongst boys and therefore, with disgust and jealousy, by the girls.

Once her parents came to know that their daughter was on the way of becoming the next whore in the brothel, they decided to get her married. Unlike what they had thought, Uma agreed immediately with the marriage. It did not matter to her that the man in question was illiterate and a foot shorter than her; for all that mattered to Uma was to get the red line on her head and the black thread around her neck. With that, she had assumed, came liberty to use her body with no restrictions. Uma wanted to fly. Marriage was just her way of getting her own pair of brand new wings.

****

Constable Tatya with his pants rolled up to his knees and fanning himself with his cap were ominous signs. PI Gaurang parked his bullet and walked up to his tired constable. As he started to stand up, Gaurang motioned to him to stay put. The constable saluted him and continued fanning his profusely sweating face. A casual question and Gaurang found himself racing back to his bike. Even before the constable could formulate what had happened, PI Gaurang Sahib was out of the compound and on his way to the municipal hospital. He hoped against hope, that the body discovered was not of the person he thought it was.

Like a couple of others, he had received the description of the clothes she was last seen in. A sensation of fear and elation grew in his heart and he was strangely frightened that the others would know just how he was feeling… hopeful. And they matched with those found on the body which had been fished out that morning. If it was so, then he needed to act fast. He cursed his inapt wife in his mind for having caused the delay; he had to curse someone.

****

The doctor could not be least bothered about yet another dead person. It sounded insensitive, but Dr. Sagar Hegde did not have time for a postmortem. The body could wait a couple of hours more. There was no facility for preserving a dead body with this level of decomposition. The stench was overbearing and the ward boy had requested the doctor to do away with it, for the third time, that day. But the doctor's OPD was overflowing with patients with different levels of morbidity. He had a woman in labor, and a child with probable tetanus.

After he had dismissed the ward boy for the third time, he set on to examine the woman in labour. By his judgment, the woman should have delivered several hours ago. A swollen spongy tissue with no evidence of the child's head alerted the doctor that he was probably dealing with an obstructed labor. With his gloves still on, he fished out the phone from his pocket and dialed the gynecologist in the Community Health Center. Confirming her presence and willingness to have the woman in the hospital, Dr. Hegde proceeded to have the tired and fatigued woman transferred to the secondary care center as soon as was possible for him.

As he wheeled her to the Public Health Center's only ambulance, with a concerned husband in tow, he was forced to retch as the doors were opened to accommodate the patient. In spite of the valiant efforts of the driver of having washed the van and mopped it with copious amounts of Dettol, the smell was overbearing. But none of it seemed to bother the tired patient as she kept drifting in and out of consciousness.

Dr. Sagar knew that she might not make it to the hospital which was situated 50kms from there. He knew that probably keeping the patient with him and trying unconventional methods of delivery might have given her better odds at survival; he had to send her off to avoid medico-legal consequences. As the doors of the van closed and the driver drove off, he could not help but feel guilty. But then, he saw the long line outside the OPD and decided to keep guilt and shame at bay.

He had learned to compartmentalize his feelings, because, without that he had discovered, that life as the only qualified doctor in a PHC was not only difficult, but impossible. He jogged off to his OPD, passing the make shift morgue on his way. The whiff of stale putrid air reminded him of the long due postmortem, but it could wait. Whoever she was, she was way beyond his help.

CHAPTER FIVE

First day of marriage

Mahesh was twenty nine. That made him a decade older than his "brand new" wife. It was one of the many things which made him wish that he was not sitting there on the rickety bed while his wife was sitting expectantly, covered from head to toe in her marriage attire. He was not nervous, he was defeated. The whole rigmarole of going through all the rituals and bearing the uncomfortable clothes had made him tired and edgy. The food lay in his stomach like a load of bricks. His weak stomach was grunting and growling throwing up belches every now and then.

He knew what was expected of him tonight and he was not a bit up to the job. Yet, he did not want to start his new life with an unsatisfied wife. He waited for things to quieten both outside the room and inside his stomach. Once he was sure that all of his drunken cousins and brothers had left or fallen unconscious, he decided to start a conversation with Uma. He removed his ridiculous head dress and increased the speed of the table fan which had come with the bride. The fan whirled merrily making it's still on plastic wrapper to rustle.

It drew a laugh from his wife. Mahesh, already sweating profusely, suddenly found his clothes had been on for longer than he had bargained for. He skipped the jacket whose synthetic interior lining spattered with static electricity. The bride laughed some more. Mahesh wondered, if she was laughing at him or the funny noises that he had been producing.

Nevertheless, once out of his jacket and having cooled off a little by the table fan, he decided to have a look at his wife for the first time. He walked up to where she was sitting and tried to remove her pallu, as he had seen in movies. To his annoyance, he discovered that, unlike movies, in real life, it required at least a hundred pins to hold the pallu artistically over the head. As he unintentionally yanked off a couple of pins, the bride decided to take matters in her own hand. Gently, she removed the inexperienced hands of her naïve husband and started removing each pin slowly and patiently. Mahesh found himself counting the pins and discovered that there were a total of twenty five pins, in and around her hair. With a final pull, Uma let the sheer piece of red fabric slip off her head.

Mahesh looked at her in awe. He had never seen a woman in his life from this close a distance. Some of the makeup had dissolved, not able to withstand the heat. The contrast between the tones in her face and neck did not seem to bother Mahesh. He was taken in by the huge eyes and the naughty twinkle in them. He did not know what to do next. While he sat dumbly staring at her with his hands clutching the edge of the bed, Uma knew, that she might have to be the one to decide, choose, and initiate everything for her husband from that day on. The feeling of power was intoxicating.

Uma straightened up. Slowly she started to remove her jewelry one piece at a time, never once taking her eyes off her man. The act was a short one, as her poor father had been able to get her only a nose ring, necklace and a pair of earrings. The black threaded necklace with two dime sized gold discs had been from her in laws. She decided to keep her red bangles and silver anklets on. She removed the pins holding her saree in place. She then patted herself from head to toe, making sure that there were no missed sentinels which could poke or hurt her anyone.

Then, she got off the bed and lifted her hand off the saree which had been draped carefully to cover her cleavage. The saree dropped off with a rustle and gathered around her feet. Mahesh looked at the woman with the large eyes, her neck ending at an impossible length at her chest.

The green blouse was cut modestly but did nothing to conceal the discernible swell of her breasts. Neither was the half draped saree doing anything to conceal the smooth contour of her flat abdomen dipping and rising at the right places, just to hide behind the pleated covers.

Uma felt her pulse rising. The way this man was looking at her was making her feel dizzy. There was a sudden warmth which had crept up in her body which spread all over her body and seemed to have congregated somewhere on her chest. Suddenly the garment felt un-comfortable… unnecessary at best. As she moved towards Mahesh, he straightened himself, his hands bunched up into fists, undecided about what to do next.

Uma was done with waiting. She took his strangely rigid hands and priced the fingers apart, one by one. The clamminess of his palms told her that he was nervous; but he did not pull back when she placed both his hands on her burning chest. When he did nothing else, she pushed herself against his hands. Mahesh did not need any more encourage-ment. He did not even wait to remove the interrupting blouse, so badly he wanted to touch and feel the elusive breasts he had often fantasized about. He felt her harden up immediately.

He dared to look up at the face of this goddess of beauty who had decided to bless the rest of his life with her body. He should not have looked up, because then he could do nothing about the way he pulled off the flimsy bit of cloth, and touched the pink reds of her breast; marveling at the way they stiffened and softened in tune with his touch.

Uma pressed in closer as the touch wasn't enough. She struggled out of the blouse, and out of habit, brought her hair to the front, in the process covering herself completely up to the midriff. Mahesh, disagreeing to anymore barriers, pushed the curtain of heavy and wavy hair from her right breast and gave in to the lifelong temptation of tasting this exotic fruit. He loved the way it hardened in his mouth. His tongue found her nipple and teased it, succeeding in drawing a moan from his wife. He felt empowered as she held his head closer to him as he took most of her breast in his mouth and sucked on it; all the while priming her left one.

When he finally let go off the right breast, he stood up and kissed Uma on her mouth, uncaring for the bright red lipstick applied carefully on the luscious lips. The flavor of strawberry filled his mouth. He mentally noted to remember this remarkable night with the woman with strawberries. But that was for later. Now, all he wanted was to pick her up and place her on his lap, while his mouth found the left sided treat. He found the string tied around her waist which was holding up her petticoat and the rest of her bunched up 9 yards.

The knot was complex and it only tightened as he pulled on it. Uma found a quick solution by snapping it off with a tug; and off came her saree and she was standing on his thigh with the help of her knee. Visibly, new underwear designed to look alluring covered the triangle between her legs. But Mahesh's courage had given up altogether. He had neither read nor imagined anything further than kissing a woman or touching her breasts. He was going crazy with the incessant throbbing in his pants. He now realized why his brother had insisted on underwear. It was all that was stopping him from squirting all over her.

Suddenly Uma climbed off his lap, and for one agonizing moment Mahesh thought that she had already given up on him. But then he was relieved, as she tossed her hair off her shoulders, square up her shoulders and took off the unaccustomed garment off in one sweep. Then, she pushed him on the bed, which rocked dangerously at being treated so roughly for the first time in its life. Mahesh took cue and removed his sheaths of clothes, quickly, not as sensually as Uma.

His penis sprang out from its confines and did not have even a minute to take in its liberty when his bride came up to him, and circled her hands around his neck. Then she slid her body over his as she climbed on him and encircled her strong legs around his waist, taking him into her soft and welcomingly wet body as easily as it had been made just for this moment. It was Mahesh's turn to moan as this exotic woman drove him out of his senses. He was afraid he would fall if he did not lie down and so he kneeled on his knees and placed Uma on the bunch of discarded clothes, making a soft makeshift bed for her.

And then, with him already in her they started the rhythm of life, which is in-built in all humans, something which needs not be taught, which is as natural as eating or drinking, but which is unmatched to any other primal needs. Perhaps because it is not only a need, but the defi-nition of life; the basis on which the human race thrives. He pushed himself deeper and faster in her body, making her arch herself almost in a sitting position, her head thrown back into ecstasy and abandon, as she gave her body unabashed to her husband and took in his with the rights of being his woman.

The difference in age, the mismatch in color, the absence of any comfort or luxury became immaterial. Mahesh thought he could stay like this for as long as she wanted, and Uma to her delight found that he could. And so, two people, who had never seen each other, and who had been arranged to be together, discovered each other, and declared their ownership. Mahesh had already vowed his life and everything he had to this damsel, while Uma made sure, that her man was never go-ing to go anywhere else. They made love a couple of times more, each more charged than the last. The bed was fortunately left unused as it would have been awkward to explain a broken bed to people.

CHAPTER SIX

Identity Issues

Dr. Sagar Hegde could not postpone the autopsy any longer. The cocky police inspector with newly decorated two stars on his shoulder had been audacious enough to scare off the remaining patients in the Outpatient Department and outside. He had insisted on sitting in his office while he told off the last patient. It was evident to him, that this was an important case which had the potential to kick up murk stinker that itself. With the inspector in the health center, even the ward boys had become smug and confident.

The doctor knew who the boss was. A disagreement would only result into another transfer to another obscure, off the map, village. And the doctor was no more interested, having learnt it the hard way. In the last ten years, crude politics and the stunted growth of his salary compared to his less read and competent friends, had made his passion and concern for the patients a joke. What mattered was living through each day by not getting lynched, stabbed, or ambushed; till the end of the month when his measly salary ringed its arrival in his mobile.

Several times he had attempted to break through and try and get a job elsewhere but had been unfortunate for having been on scholarship from the Government which had supported him through his specialization in medicine. He had a fourteen year deal with the Government which he could not breech. At the time when he was offered the scholarship, it had seemed like the bright light at the end of the tunnel.

A year into the field as the Medical Officer in a Public Health Center, he had realized that it was not the light, but the tunnel itself; filled with garbage and rodents. The light grew dimmer with each passing year, and now into the tenth year, it had dwindled into a feeble glimmer.

Dr. Sagar sighed. He knew he had to get up right then and carry out the autopsy. He was surprised when the inspector insisted on being present. Sagar did not object. He had learnt to never give his opinion; it was the last thing anyone wanted. He shrugged his shoulders and invited the PI to feel at home and do whatever he fancied. After gearing himself with as many masks as he could lay his hands on, he entered the room where the body was kept on the stretcher and shrouded with a white cloth.

The stench hit him like a punch. He had amputated gangrenous limbs and removed retained placentas in illegal abortions done by quacks. He had removed loads of feces from morbidly obese patients and treated patients pouring watery diarrhea in cholera wards. But none of that had prepared him for this miasma. The inspector, not finding any mask in the steel drum had used his handkerchief instead. He could not make it beyond the door and doubled up vomiting in his handkerchief. The doctor, gaining a sadistic pleasure in the PI's discomfort, left him to his fate, and proceeded with the autopsy.

There was not much left of the body. It was impossible to identify her as all her worthy features had been chewed off by some hungry fish. Her fingers, were another story altogether. The doctor donned gloves as he examined the fingers. At a first glance they seemed like an act of the aquatic life, but then the proximal phalange had been neatly sawed to the middle of the bone… each ten of them. The purple natural tattoo on her neck made it very clear that she had been strangled ante mortem. The doctor concluded that the killer or killers had not taken into account that the rope they were using would leave its marks as clear on her neck as if it was still there.

He slightly tilted on the side and neatly cut away the blouse. A close inspection showed nothing more than wrinkled skin which had peeled in several places. There were no birth marks he could make out. The body was so decomposed that chunks of flesh came off in his hands. Sagar quickly made a note of things which were evident. He was not expected to do a detailed analysis at the PHC but he was responsible to inform the authorities and tertiary care center if he found something fishy. He removed each piece of clothing and labeled it. The intestines which had been protruding from the burst abdomen were lying stubbornly coiled in purple-gray loops.

The sparse jewelry was removed with a wire cutter and labeled. The doctor noted three toe rings and concluded that the woman must have been married. But not only were the rings on the toes bejeweled, they were made of gold… and that meant only one thing: affluence. Once the preliminary procedure was done, he wrapped up the body into a white sheet.

As a foot note, he added that the woman was found with a posthumously delivered fetus which was about eight months in the stage of development. Would he have lived if delivered naturally? Probably yes. He jotted in the form, and once the last detail had been entered, he automatically signed on the dotted line, and authorized it with a stamp stating its authenticity. Then, handling the visibly shaken and sick looking PI the report, he walked off to his bike even without breaking his step. With not even the courtesy of a look, he drove off to his house, dying to peel off his clothes, and hopefully the gory image of the poor dead woman from his mind.

****

Ratan Macchi was washing the clothes he had worn to the cremation ground. It was the only other pair of clothes he owned which were not torn. He tried to rub off the red stain from the cheap earthen pot on his shirt. The mark wouldn't come off. He rubbed it vigorously. His late wife Phooli would have removed it in a jiffy. But Phooli was gone, leaving him poorer than he ever had been. Ratan threw down the blue soap and clutched his knees in an embrace as uncontrolled sobs racked his body. How will he ever live without coming back home to her sweet voice and smile? How was he ever going to forget the first day he had seen her in the fish market haggling with a man double her size? Where will he find such feisty wife, who had filled up all the holes in his life with light and made him as complete as the fenestrated lamp she lighted every night? He looked at his pathetic shirt lying crumpled and tortured with the glaring red stain, picked it up and rinsed it in the tub of water. Then he took it out, squeezed out the moisture, and hung it on the rope besides his fishing net. He would treasure the shirt, he had decided. The mark would remind him of his Phooli… in this life and after.

****

The man was on his fourth beedi. He had been standing there behind the neem tree for the better part of the day. He had been instructed to see if Ratan Macchi made any suspicious move. Did he show agitation? Did he speak to anyone about his wife's sudden death? Did he make a move in the direction of the police station, or worse, towards the Lord's house? The man had inquired discreetly to find out if Ratan had the slightest doubt about his wife's death. He had succeeded considerably, he thought, as he had reached a conclusion which his master would be pleased with.

It was evident that Ratan had missed the slight mark of the rope around Phooli's neck. As such, the man concluded, that she was already dying when he had just given her the necessary push while he had tightened the rope around her neck. Actually, he had been rather disappointed as she died quickly without a fight or as much as a scream. Not like the last one. All eight months of pregnant and cornered by four men, she had not given up easily. She had kicked one of his men in his balls and almost scratched the life out of the other. She would have probably even struggled and fought back some more, had it not been for him.

He had had enough of the vixen and her antics. He had choked her and pulled on the rope until he could see the whites of her eyes filling up with red spots from bursting capillaries. He had pulled until her lifeless body had flopped and was practically hanging; the noose snagging into her chin just behind her ears. He was sorry when she had died. He had always liked this one best. Over the years a sort of friendship had developed between them. He had also broken the rule of not getting emotionally involved with any of them, and he had let her tie a 'rakhi' on his wrist, taking a vow from him to protect her in all circumstances. But what she hadn't realized was that his master was bigger to him than any relationship. So, when he was commanded to do away with her, he hadn't even batted an eye.

CHAPTER SEVEN

Hidden in Shadows

PI Gaurang had removed the last traces of vomitus from his uniform. He would rather be dead than allow his wife the satisfaction of seeing his weakness. He had used up all the water from his flask to rinse out the acid and bile from his mouth. His soiled handkerchief had been thrown unceremoniously on the ground and kicked out of the way.

After regaining his composure, he read the report handed to him by the obnoxious doctor. He made a mental note of dealing with the smug later. First, he needed to get the most important things done. He needed to ensure everything was in order. The idiot had missed the fingers… all the more better. The report was ok, except for the last part where the fetus was mentioned. He would have to ask the doctor to remove that unnecessary point as no one would be hurt by the reduced info.

Nevertheless, he pocketed the report, and hopped on his bike. Time to meet Charu… but then, the smell emitting from his clothes was repulsive even to him. He could not let Charu turn up her beautiful nose and kick him out of her house. Maybe it was not the time to meet her. Disheartened and disappointed, he made his way reluctantly towards his home. He would have to also make do with homemade food today.

At home, he was irked by just the fact that his pathetic wife had been waiting for him at the door steps. And when she saw him, she rushed to him like a bloody servant and took his flask and tiffin box. Later, she followed him around like a dog with a glass of water, a towel, and a fresh pair of clothes…. He hated this clueless woman absent of spine. He loved adventure… a touch of danger; in his work, and also in his women.

He had been with countless women both before and after his marriage to this dud; but never had he been burnt the way Charu's beauty and fire had burnt him. So taken was he with her magic that every woman seemed to pale in comparison. He had always disliked his wife, and now with Charu in his life, she did not even stand half a chance.

He finished the meal she brought, grudgingly agreeing in his mind that it was delicious. He washed his hands in the plate itself with the water Lata poured out for him. He knew that she would throw out the water and eat in the same plate, just as she had been doing for the last few years. Then he went to his room and decided to sleep. But sleep was sparse tonight.

His unmet desire of being with Charu and have her make love to him was not letting him sleep. He tried several things to settle his engorged penis. He tried to masturbate with the help of saucy porn. He tried to imagine Charu and her gorgeous jingling breasts as she rode him and simultaneously flicking herself; but the thoughts and visualization only made his erection harder to get over with. He had only one way of dealing with it.

He went back to the veranda where Lata was washing the utensils. Gaurang forced himself to look at her milky white legs with her saree rolled up to avoid getting wet. He mentally ripped off her head and replaced it with that of Charu… now there was not much difference. He walked up to her and tapped on her shoulder. She almost died of fright as she stood up, upsetting the stacked utensils, mixing the washed and the unwashed ones.

Gaurang motioned her to come inside the house. Once she was barely in, he pulled up her saree and petticoat and forced her to part her legs. The salt and cheese of her vagina was tingled with a hint of rose. Lata, finding herself in such close intimacy with her husband for the first time in a long time, could not help but spread her legs further and voluntarily. She put her hands on his shoulder for balance as he kept digging her further and further with his tongue.

Then without any warning, he stood up and turned her, holding her up against the wall, her saree still bunched high above her waist. Then he entered her from behind and thrust relentlessly, slamming her body again and again against the hard wall. Lata came out of her momentary dream into the real world… having her husband rape her once again. She knew that he would continue until she bled. He would continue to dig his fingers into her tender breasts until he was satisfied that there were nail marks on them.

She started the process of numbing her brain and abandoning her body for the coming hour as he raved and clawed her flesh. She forced her mind to think of the child she would have one day, and the love she would shower on him. She closed her eyes and imagined getting her little one ready for school. She pictured tying her daughter's hair in plaits. She imagined getting them married and seeing grandchildren….

Tears rolled off the corners of her eyes as her physical pain and humiliation drove the pleasant thoughts out of her mind, and she knew that none of it was going to happen… because she would probably die before that.

When the man had finished, she stood up and staggered out of the room, her saree still hitched above her waist. She walked to the bathroom and took a pail of water, and doused her vagina.

The cool water felt like acid on her bruised genitals. Still, she kept dousing, until the blood stopped, and the water returned clean. Then she rolled a cloth and tied it around her vulva to take up the bleeding. Once that was in place, she walked back to the utensils and squatted to finish the washing the dishes. She would need them in the morning to serve breakfast to her husband.

****

Dr. Sagar Hegde drove as fast as he could with his motorcycle on the dirt road. The solitary street lamp flickering as if trying to stay awake was the only source of light in the dark. Judging the distance of the nearest pothole from the lamp, he decided to ride on the edge of the road to avoid painful surprises. His house was situated about 30 kilometers from the Public Health Center.

Every day, he had to make his way back to his house through a comparatively unmanned road. While the sparsity of vehicles made it an uninterrupted ride, it was an ideal place to get ambushed. It had been several years that the doctor had been making these solitary journeys to and fro, and had never encountered anything more viscous than a rat snake. The mundane ride put the doctor in a pensive mood.

The decomposed, and partially eaten human remains he had just written a report on was in all certainty a murder, and the presence of the Police Inspector himself confirmed the hands of big shots at work. The biggest hand he could think of was the self-proclaimed God-man living in a plush three tiered house on the sea side, who went by the name: the Lord. Always preposterously dressed in white, with a garland of red roses, he seemed as phony to the doctor as the autopsy report he had just signed and stamped.

Something resembling guilt started creeping up his gut. He had intentionally omitted the mention of the chopped off fingers. He knew, that if he had mentioned that or any slight possibility of the death being any other thing except accidental, he would have to start expecting unpleasant encounters on this stretch of road. The people could go to any lengths and depths to hide their secrets. Everyone else who was placed on the altar was just collateral damage. The doctor knew that except the rulers and movers, everyone else was expendable.

Today, for some unknown reason he wasn't feeling the level of sanguinity he allowed himself as soon as he was out of the PHC. The feeling of impending doom and trepidation was increasing by each kilometer he closed up towards his house. He tried to shake off the feeling in vain. He could see the colony gate. A little further on, and he could make out his quarter.

Something made him stop his bike suddenly. He applied the brakes, and switched off the ignition. The faint light from the bike faded, covering the doctor in a protective darkness. Everything was as it always was. The flimsy gate, hanging from its hinges was unmanned as usual. The lights were off except for a few zero watt bulbs glowing like a demon's eyes.

Once his eyes adjusted to the darkness; he looked intently at his slightly ajar front door. He remembered something similar happened to the doctor posted before him. He had just written an honest report, and did his duty of informing the police. The next day when he did not report for duty, the cleaner decided to give him a home call. It was very unusual for the doctor to miss any day at work. The cleaner had found the door unlocked and the doctor hanging from the ceiling fan, a small table, upturned under him. A case of suicide was registered almost immediately, and the unmarried status of the doctor made the reason for his extreme step. His file was effectively buried deep amongst the others and the spot was filled up with another doctor.

Sagar was no fool. He was quick to disembark and push his bike off the road as soon as he could. He dragged it to the fork in the road and only then, when he was sure that he had the advantage of distance, he kick-started his bike and drove away in the opposite direction as fast as he could. He had no intensions, whatsoever, to be another file lost in oblivion.

CHAPTER EIGHT

What Makes the Man

It had been just another hot sweltering day. Dhaniram was waiting on the railway tracks, every now and then touching them to gauze the distance of the incoming train. He knew that a goods freight train used to pass the village at the dead of night, at about 2 am. Today, it had been late. Dhaniram cursed his luck. Even in death, God had decided to play a joke on him. Of all the nights, He had decided to choose this particular one to delay the train.

Dhaniram had come prepared. A bottle of toddy had given him the courage to mince himself by standing in front of an upcoming train. He had taken care of the rest of the family… his wife and his four children, would never go hungry anymore. No more snatching at each other's bread; no more cribbing for more rice.

His poverty stricken mind had given him the twisted idea that feeding all of them one last meal laced with rat poison was the only thing he could do to satisfy his perpetually hungry family. He had waited till the last of them had stopped breathing. The eldest had taken the longest time to die and Dhaniram had helped him by choking out his last breaths. After that, he had shrouded all five of them and locked the door from outside. Then he had walked all the way to the station, and waited for the train.

Dhaniram had waited for the whole night, and eventually, fallen asleep by the tracks. When he opened his eyes, he hoped that all of it had been a dream. The reek of poison from his clothes and hands told him otherwise. The horror of what he had done came upon him and he could not bear to face himself. Sorrow quickly changed to guilty and guilt into the fear of getting caught.

His guilt ridden mind mirrored everyone looking at him. It seemed to him that everyone could read his mind, and knew what he had done. For four days he stayed put on the by lanes in the tunnel, trying to wish death upon himself. The image of his children laughing and hugging him changed to their blue dead faces rapidly. So many times, he willed himself to stand in front of the racing train. But then, as days passed by, the images turned blurry. A comforting thought had taken place of the guilt and fear.

Dhaniram reasoned that had God wished him to die, he would have been dead by now, hundred times over. The fact that the freight train had been cancelled that day itself meant that God had blessed him with a long life. Empowered by this new thought, Dhaniram, with his beard and over grown hair masking his identity, climbed inside the next train and surrendered his future to fate. He decided that the train would take him where he needed to be. So, when the next day, the train pulled up in the small town of Dahanu, Dhaniram stepped down on the platform, deciding to claim the town as his own.

In a country where each person is trying to bribe some sort of God to put his matters in selfish order, the easiest thing is to become a saint. It is common knowledge, even amongst the average minded men like Dhaniram, that each person, rich, poor or anywhere in between, wanted two things in life: to be appreciated, and to be told that how they have been wronged by others. A look at a face or palm, followed by a speech using the two sentences as a mantra in a heavy dreamy baritone, was enough to convince the sanest that they were in the company of the only man on the earth who could understand them.

Soon, it was known far and wide, that there was an enlightened young soul who could look beyond. Dhaniram upgraded his sermons to include his rudimentary knowledge about the

Mahabharat and Ramayan, which he had seen on television. Generic statements said with the right panacea and elocution was bound to be right. The trick was to buy a man's soul by feeding it the much needed praise, and then validating all his actions, both good and bad. Soon, Dhaniram became Dhayanand Baba.

Later, even this identity of an elevated man also became typical… way beyond the level of reverberation the people showed him. It was only a matter of years that the despair driven murderer, became The Lord himself. And with the title came impossible power; power to play with the minds of the mere mortals; power to make the sinful acts of devotion; power to make people ready to barter their souls for a mere corroboration of their acts. By the time Dhaniram became The Lord, he had that kind of power over the port and the numerous villages based on the shore of the picturesque beach.

It was this power that made him an important link in the chain of deceit growing stronger and viler than ever. Often, The Lord wondered, that if he, a murderer, a con-man and a convict was just a lower rung in the ladder, what kind of dead conscience did those right on the top have? He was a smart man, and long back he had stopped asking questions when he had found a cutting of an old newspaper describing the ruthless murders of five people in a family, used as a wrapping for some anonymous money donated to his Ashram. Whoever they were, they knew everything… and wanted him to know nothing.

✳✳✳✳✳✳✳✳✳✳✳✳

The man was nervous. He knew that the news of the escape of the doctor would not be taken lightly. He was unable to fathom where he had gone wrong. He had picked the cheap lock and slipped inside the house, with no one being wiser. He had waited in the dark like a shadow. He had guessed the tentative time of the doctor's return and was ready for him. He had been right spot on, in all his deductions till now. Like clockwork, the doctor's bike stopped at the gate.

The man was ready with the slender length of nylon in his hand, pulled taut to be wound around the neck and held tight till the breath stopped. The excitement of the act was making him edgy. Last time, it had been so easy. The man had surmised that the old doctor had died of a heart attack, rather than his never failing rope. The previous job had been planned with a little time in hand. But this time, the boss had given him no time to plan. He had to improvise.

The thick bush which had given him a nice vantage the last time had been chopped off. So he had to keep the door slightly ajar to keep an eye on his victim. As he had expected, the bike stopped right at gate. But then something strange happened. The doctor took a prompt turn and went the other way. Running after him would be risky and hopeless, considering the disadvantage of him being on foot. However fit he was, he was no match for a motorcycle. It was certain that the doctor was smarter than given credit for. The only thing which must have given him away was the slightly ajar door.

Disappointed and frightened, he dialed the boss's number. As usual, the soft voice, dangerously deceitful, just replied with an ok. The man was not a fool and could feel the undercurrent of rage in the simple answer. It was time to disappear for a few days. But where could he go? The answer disheartened him further. Nowhere… there was nowhere he could hide… nor could the doctor.

****

Sagar looked at the fuel meter. The dial was turning to the red mark with astonishing speed. He was nowhere near any safe destination. When he had realized that his quarters had been opened and infiltrated, his first instinct was to run… just run. Where? That he would decide on his way of escape. As soon as he had put some kilometers between himself and the to-be killer, his heartbeat returned to a bit of its normal rate.

He thought hard for a place to go. There were no safe friend's or family's place he could turn to. And the fact that he was not having the advantage of distinguishing friends from enemies was making his options slimmer. The bike started to sputter as the last drop of the petrol in the reserve dried up after giving one last push to the piston. The inertia pushed the dead automobile for a few meters and Sagar utilized the push to ride the bike close to a nearby bush. He parked it on its stand and looked around. He was in middle of nowhere.

There was no milestone or any billboard… not even a measly tea stall anywhere in sight. He looked around haplessly. He had very little money on him. All his clothes and sparse belongings were in the house he could not go back to… at least, not yet. But morning might be safer. He decided to camp on the roadside for the night. He spread his handkerchief on the grass and leaned on his bike. The warmth from the silencer was comforting.

He removed his phone and noticed gloomily, that there was no reception. Sagar closed his eyes and thought, why had he been pulled into this muck. Fourteen years of education, innumerable sleepless nights, and countless patients treated… what had his diligence and selflessness earned him… the sterling opportunity of becoming a pawn?

The shrill ringing of his phone pulled him out of his sleep in a jolt. For a moment Sagar thought that he had been cornered. Who in the hell knew where he was? Then, he realized that his phone was still with him and had a single bar making it possible for someone to reach him. His despair turned to relief when he saw the name flashing across the screen. Why hadn't he thought of her?

He picked up the call and listened to the one minute long single sided string of complaints which ended with a genuine concern in the voice. Sagar retold his story and also the reason why he had been unreachable. The person on the other side must have been stunned into silence, because Sagar had to repeat a 'hello' several times, before she spoke up again. She wanted to know where he was, and she was coming to get him right then. A grateful Sagar shared his location, which showed that he was somewhere very near to the city. He was amazed at how far his bike had managed to pull him away from danger. He patted the motorcycle and sat on its seat, as he started his wait for his savior and friend.

CHAPTER NINE

Bottles of Gold

Ratan did not know what to make of the tiny bottles he had found stashed away in a plastic bag at the corner of the room that serves as his kitchen, just behind the stacked blackened pots. The bottles were containing some white powder and were sealed tightly. The bottles were shaped like very tiny light bulbs. There was no label or name on them. The glasses were thick and transparent. It was the strangest thing the fisherman had ever seen in his life.

Then he took them all out of the plastic bag and counted a total of two hundred pellet-sized bottles. He had no idea what they were. His wife must have hid these in this strange place. Ratan thought it was indeed a good hiding place, and he would have never come across them, had he not been trying to get a pot from the stack.

He dropped all the 200 bottles in the bag and tightly wound the plastic around it. He returned the packet back in its hiding place, and started to think what he was supposed to do next. But what were these bottles doing in his hut? He knew it couldn't be salt nor sugar… and it was nothing like anything he had seen used for fishing. Then, as if waking from a dream, a strange thought came to his mind. For several minutes he just sat there in the cold kitchen staring ahead of him.

Was that possible… his own Phooli? Impossible… but there was only one way to find out. He fished out the packet once again and took out one of the bottles. He placed it on the floor and stood on his with his slippers on. He put all his weight on the foot, but the bottle remained unscratched. He tried throwing it on the ground, but it only bounced a little bit and then rolled, unbroken, in a corner.

Rattan was not to be dissuaded so easily. He looked around for something heavy with which he could beat the obstinate bottle. He located a mortar and piston. He took the bottle and placed it the mortar and brought the piston down on it with a crash. The resilient bottle held on for a couple of blows, before it gave way with a slight crack. Ratan took a piece of paper and poured the sparkling white powder on it.

Gingerly, he separated the pieces of glass and put them aside. The powder was strangely alluring. A few rays of the sun made the dust-like powder sparkle. A memory, suppressed in the recess of his mind, reappeared. Long back, very long back, he had seen a similar kind of powder. He took a pinch of it and placed it on his tongue. The strangely floral smell and the bitter tart taste tinged his senses and transported him into a world without pain, grief or sorrow. This world of euphoria, left behind long back ago, told him exactly what was there in the bottles.

He had seen the powder in a different container, at a different place, being used for a different purpose. When the induced high had lifted off, Ratan's mind started throbbing with questions. Could these bottles explain why his Phooli became so sick all of a sudden? Could it explain the pangs of pain which strangled her body and ravaged it in the end? Could it explain her sudden devotion to the Lord? His mind told him that it was all possible. The only thing not possible was to die the way she did. That meant that her death had been augmented by human hands. And that also meant that whoever it was, knew about the bottles, and where they likely were. The only thing they might not have foreseen was that someone as simple as a fisherman would know what they were.

By instinct, Ratan got up and picked up the pieces of glass he had broken. He held them in the cup of his palm and dropped a few drops of water on it. The sharp edges dropped down as if made of jelly. He pinched the substance between his fingers and discovered that his deductions were correct. Ratan was in the possession of hundreds of vials of the purest form of cocaine, packed in pellets of hard glass like substance, almost too hard to break, but pliable enough to swallow when taken with water.

There was no doubt in his mind now that his wife had been a mule. And like the occasional accidents when a malfunctioning pellet burst open in the stomach flooding it with unaccustomed high at times more than often, the mule gets addicted; and therefore a liability instead of an asset. And the worlds within which the cocaine was being switched for inconceivable money, there was no place for inconsequential liabilities like Phooli.

****

Mahesh could not have enough of her. She was fiery, and nothing shamed her. She did not blush, but changed into an exotic color of fresh honey whenever she climaxed. Inattentive to the attention her moans and cries were getting outside the closed door, she continued to push Mahesh to limits which he himself was unaware of. She was unstoppable, and Mahesh was not sure, that he wanted her to stop at all. So, it was with lots of reluctance that they got dressed and came out of their exotic confines, when the mother of the dazzled groom rattled the door incessantly, in an effort to stop the orgy.

The new bride, her body simmering with the sweat of hours of unbridled love making, came out of the room, her head covered all the way to the top of her face and her saree bunched up an inch higher than required. She walked the compound, her long firm legs ramping up and ending each sensual step with a jingle of her anklet. She surveyed her arena coyly from under her pallu, held in place with red henna clad hands. She could feel the collective heat being emitted from all the brothers, cousins, uncles, and fathers who had gathered in the compound under the pretext of having their breakfast and tea. But

Uma knew exactly what they had come to feast on. She moved across the veranda, feeling all the eyes, both male and female, on her. She took painfully long time to reach the other end of the house.

Once there, this woman all of nineteen years of age, turned towards the direction of the kitchen in such a way, that the wind caught her pallu and slipped it off her head and bosom. It was only natural that she would blush with all of her brothers-in-law now gazing at her womanhood, and gave out a sigh. But Mahesh, sitting amidst the onlookers knew that his wife never blushed… the rising color was his nymph getting ready to be loved again.

CHAPTER TEN

Assassins'

The boss was irritated. They did not make the assassins as they used to in good old days. Silent, passive, and efficient to the point of impossible; the yesteryears had seen the perfect killers. Their work was so superlative…no unnecessary force or violence…not a drop of blood more than required. The boys now-a-days were crazy. Most of them were mentally deranged in various degrees. Killing was not a profession for them, it was a sport. The murkier and messier they could make it, the more fun they derived from it. Because they had big God-fathers standing behind them, they did not find it imperative to clean up after them.

The boss, instead of concentrating on other things was busy being a nanny to the blue-collar sods who called themselves assassins. The doctor had been way too smart. He had escaped the net… or that is what he must be thinking. The boss knew him… he knew that the doctor had seen everything and registered them all in his head. The doctor could not be bought… he could not be cajoled…. The boss knew that it was only a matter of time before he would join the dots and become immediately expendable. But, for today, he could live. As such being the boss was not for unnecessary manslaughter. It was always difficult and time consuming to hide the blood trails.

The inspector had called. The Lord had called. From their collective information it was very clear that they had found her. It was her alright... the boss knew. The toe rings were unique and one of their kind. She would change each piece of jewelry on her body every single day, but the toe rings stayed. She had insisted on the gold ones and had them custom made. Years of adornment, had made removing the rings impossible. The idiots had had the idea of chopping off her toes as well, like her fingers, before they pushed her into the sea. Again, like irascible children, they had called the boss to tell that they had had the brain-storm a moment too late.

The boss had no time for inaptitude. There were many more matters to sort out. The sea rarely threw out her kills… and the boss trusted the sea more than his men. But she had been hot tempered and grumpy lately… and decided to act like the bitch she used to be once in a while.

The inspector had made sure that the autopsy report was as vague as it could be. Yet, there was the mention of the fetus. That needed to be removed. On second thought, it did not really matter that much now. Yes, the pregnancy had been an unpleasant surprise. But just as there was not a single living soul in the world who was concerned about the dead, half eaten woman found in the sea, no one cared for the unborn child. Again, the boss had a second look at the report and decided that it would do. After all, who would want to read the report? By the end of the day, she will be cremated along with the child and the story will end right there.

There will be no loose threads, no frayed ends; except maybe, for the doctor. But this guy had been much more practical than the previous one. He had realized that staying alive was much more important and fruitful than being scrupulously honest. The previous doctor's honesty edged onto being nosey. He had come too close to the truth. The boss sort of liked the new doctor. With a little bit of tutoring, he could be turned into an asset. The problem was that he was on the run, understandably so… but the boss needed to know where he was. Whether to recruit him or to kill him, well, that was up to the doctor, wasn't it?

****

Revathi was driving at 20 km/hr; looking out of the window, intently, for any sign of life. Her phone kept telling her that her destination was on the right… then it prompted her to take a U-turn, and then her destination was on her left. She crossed the same spot at least four times before she had the bright idea to call on his cell phone. She got a reception and the phone rang. She could hear the phone somewhere nearby.

She drove in the general direction of the sound, one hand on the steering and the other holding her own phone as a guide. After several other futile attempts, the irate reporter parked her car by the road side and decided to find her friend on foot. The unattended ringing phone was making her edgy. She dialed the number again and this time, she could hear the ringing very close by. She walked a little further into the bushes and came face to face with the weirdest thing she had ever seen.

In the clearing, a long branch of a tree had been propped straight clumsily with bricks and stones supporting its base. On the top of the branch a small black object had been tied with some wire twined generously around it. The object was flashing Revathi's number and incessantly ringing. It was the doctor's phone. There was no sign of the doctor. She looked about frantically in the nearby vegetation expecting the worst. His bike was parked in a relatively shaded area on its double stands.

It was clear, that the doctor had left the scene a long time back and he had taken great pain in making sure that his phone was discovered. Revathi shook the pole and was surprised to find that it had been secured quite firmly. After struggling for a few minutes, she could manage to bend the branch low enough to get hold of the phone. Untwining it from the branch was another story altogether.

She hoped that the phone was not password protected. It was. Revathi cursed her friend profusely, assaulting the nearby bushes. Then she remembered something and fished out her own phone. She had received a very cryptic message from Sagar. The message was a jabbering long line of alphabets making no sense. When she had read it the last night, she had thought that her friend might have sat on his phone, butt-typing this erratic message.

With little hope, she entered the gibberish in Sagar's phone. She stood looking at it, astonished, as the screen came alive. The first thing she did was to disable the password protection of the phone. Next, she checked the mail. With a quickening pulse, she went on to check the whatsapp and messenger. On an impulse she opened the phone book. Revathi was really worried about her friend now.

She switched off the phone and put it in her bag. Then she switched off her phone as well… Her mind was reeling for possible answers. Why had Dr. Sagar Hegde left his phone obviously to be found by her? Where was he? And what could be the possible reason felt obliged to delete all his messages, mails, and photographs. Whatever it was, she reasoned that if the reason had been good enough for him, it was so for her as well. And maybe switching off her cell was not only what she had to do. She needed to disappear as well.

****

Why had he run? What made him hide? Hadn't he been the one to make the call? Then why did he hide when the car came his way? Had he become paranoid? Had he been watching too many crime shows? Or, had it been something he had heard …a click at the other end of the call? Had someone else being listening to their conversation? The close scrapes with death and deceit were frying up his brain. He had not slept for more than thirty-six hours. Yesterday seemed like a decade back. Maybe he was making up the problems in his head. But he decided to take his intuitions seriously. It had saved him once.

He deleted all the materials on his phone but not before he had mailed the stuff to Revathi. Somehow, he felt that the photographs might prove useful in the future in saving his life at least. Then he hid it where he knew that Revathi could find. In case she missed it, the phone was password protected and only Revathi had the password.

Parking his bike under a tree, he had secured his phone on a pole, where it got two bands of reception. And then he hid behind the thick foliage, laid flat on his stomach and waited. He saw several vehicles pass by. By the end of a painful and dusty hour, the doctor had started questioning his suspicions.

Just then, a car passed by. It was familiar. Sagar was intensely tempted to stand up and wave his hand to attract the attention of the driver. But something held him back and he continued staring at the vehicle. The vehicle crossed his field of vision several times. In different circumstances, he would have walked over to the person and accepted an offer for a ride to wherever he wanted to. But he was, instead, overcome with such dread, that he slipped a bit more into the safe camouflage of the bushes. The person in the car had rolled down the window and was looking out benignly.

To a by-looker, there may be no obvious threat in it. But Sagar knew how foolish it could be. He had trusted the wrong person. The reason why the person's presence spelt out danger for him was nothing other than the fact, that there was no way that the person could know that the doctor was here. Sagar had called his friend Revathi, and he knew she was not one to spill the beans. Therefore, the 'click' he had heard was real. Way too many people knew just where he was, with the accuracy of a few meters. It was time to run again.

CHAPTER ELEVEN

Women Ways

Inspector Gaurang had personally seen to it that the body had been cremated and the fetus thrown in together. The smell of burning putrid flesh was worse than ever. Thankfully it was over very quickly. Unlike the six to eight hours it took for an adult to be completely charred, the half liquefied body was not even an hour's work.

Once finished, he had called the boss to give the news. It was important to let the boss know exactly who it was who had done the maximum work in cleaning up the unwanted and unexpected mess. The Lord had done nothing more than smelled his ridiculous garland of roses and look on, as the police made way with the body. Next time, when it was time to meet the boss, PI Gaurang wanted to let the boss know, just who was trustworthy and who was not.

Over the last couple of years, since he had moved in into the station, he had smoothened out all the bumps on the boss's path. He had taken care of anyone with the slightest fever of rebellion in staged encounters. The few who had committed the stupid mistake of trying to steal from the Boss had found themselves at the other end of the barrel of his gun. He had done so much work for the boss, but yet, the Lord seemed to hog the lion's share of praise and money. This time, he had decided to show the phony, just who was there to stay, and who wasn't.

The sooth from the pyre had blackened his face and neck. He

splashed some water on his face and rubbed off as much ink as he could. He cursed the decision of not following his idea of keeping a fresh pair of clothes in the station. Charu had called him… she had decided to forgive him enough to grace him with the permission to visit her. He surveyed his face in the mirror and found the image unpleasing. He called out to Tatya and asked him to summon the barber. He planned to not only get a close shave and face massage; he would ask the barber to clean him up, real well 'down there' as well. More than once Charu had expressed her displeasure at having to give him a little head. The hair bothered her.

The prospects of visiting Charu had cheered him up considerably. His displeasure at being outshined by a fake God-man had disappeared the moment he saw her name displayed on his phone screen. His heart jumped to his mouth when she used her naughtiest voice to tell him that she wanted to see him; but also added that he should not expect sex. The word 'sex' from her lips were enough to arouse him. He waited for Tatya to waddle away in search of the barber. Then, he took his phone and started looking at the nudes Charu had sent him. He opened his zip and handled his penis, stroking it slowly imagining Charu's red lips around it. He came faster than he had expected. Charu always did this to him. Only if he could keep it going for longer….

****

Mahesh was gearing up for the deep sea catch. Some of the other youths had decided to join forces and paddle into the heart of the sea, expecting a good catch. The tourist season was just about to start, and the demand for the exotic fish was on the rise. Restaurants were ready to pay hefty sums for the right size of prawns and lobsters.

Uma was sitting on the bed, her legs hanging off the edge, swinging more vigorously than usual. She had been sulking for more than a week now. She did not understand why he couldn't stay with her all the time. He tried to explain that he had to work to earn his living. She had tried to seduce him to stay back and not go for the deep sea tour.

Mahesh knew, that he could well hold it off, if he wanted to. But he did not want to. He was eagerly looking out for a way to get away from his wife.

Since his marriage, Uma had become excessively aggressive and demanding. Her hunger for sexual gratification was insatiable. Initially he had insuperable desire for her. But as days passed, he realized that she was a sort of narcissist, always desiring her own pleasure. When it came to give, she was not as giving and would often pull back. Her increasing rashness and disregard for his likes and dislikes had started irking Mahesh. Within a month, the sensual beauty which had allured him stared at him with unmasked disdain.

Mahesh told himself that he should have known that things were going way too good to be true. To be fair, some of Uma's anger and disappointment had been his own doing. So strong was his subconscious desire to be away from his demanding wife that he had started distancing himself from her. The only thing he had to fall back on was fishing. He craved for the known, once again. The sea, which represented his youth and his freedom called out to him. Once out in the sea, he became a boy once again. The breeze rushing through his hair, making it unruly and roughened with the salt and humidity, was like the caress of a mother. He had been pulled, unprepared into the whirlpool of a relation which was so torrential and overwhelming, that he had lost himself. His soul urged to be found again. So, going out in the deep waters was more like getting on a lifeboat for him.

Large tears welled up in Uma's eyes. She was staring intently at the wooden bedpost and scratching the polish with her nail. After trying every trick she had up her sleeves to convince Mahesh to stay, she had taken refuge in a stubborn and absolute silence. She followed Mahesh everywhere he went, and expressed her displeasure by banging doors, or putting down utensils with more than required force. Mahesh had offered to leave her in her father's house while he was away, but Uma had just stared at him with the stoic silence which had become her favorite persona. Her ill-humor was affecting the genial aura of the house.

The rest of the members were getting jittery and annoyed as well. The generally calm household erupted into small fights and frictions over minor issues. Brothers fought, wives screamed, and the young ones became sullen and threw tantrums. It was then that a chafed Mahesh decided to take Uma to 'the factory'. In a last ditch effort to cull his volatile young wife's unpredictable anger, Mahesh thought of Keva Bai, the small time celebrity, who had played a pivotal role in bringing the name of the otherwise non-descript village on the World map. It was impossible to Google the name of the village and not read about this alpha female who had taken care of the small scale business run by her husband and in laws after their tragic demise.

Along with other ventures, she had helped the local women earn a living by teaching them the skill of making artifacts and show pieces from the sea shells which were sold at good prices as souvenirs to the tourists. The business had started from a small seaside shanty and had grown into a well-defined building with a proper office. Several of Mahesh's friends' wives were profitably employed in what the people called 'the factory'. Keva Bai was a much respected and feared woman. People of the village looked up at her with awe, as most people did when they come across a woman who did things on her own account.

Mahesh was rewiring his net when the angry jangle of anklets told him that his irked wife was standing just behind him. He geared up mentally for another meltdown. When none came, he turned and found Uma standing in front of the mirror, with a pair of shears in her hand. Then, as Mahesh looked on, she clumped a bunch of hair and chopped it off close at the scalp. She threw down the seared tresses and proceeded to continue the same with the rest of it.

Mahesh sprang up and before she could cut of another bunch of hair, he snatched the scissors from her hand and threw them far away. Uma's eyes were red with unshed tears. The part of her head where the hair had been shorn off unceremoniously looked strangely boyish. Unable to vent out her anger and disappointment in the way she seemed fit, Uma beat Mahesh on his chest with her fists. Her slight hands did not make a lot of impact, and Mahesh was inappropriately amused. His misplaced mirth earned him deep and long scratches on his arms and torso, which, hurt.

Big drops of tears started rolling from large eyes as she continued to fist his chest and wherever-else she could get her hands on. Mahesh caught hold of her hands to stop the assault. He did not realize how strongly he had clasped her wrists, nor did he notice the delicate glass bangles which had broken under his grip and had pushed their harsh sharp edges in Uma's soft wrists. A trail of bright red blood flowed from her wounds and dripped down her elbow, but she was too blinded by anger and the pain of rejection, which were more acute than the physical pain.

Mahesh held her hands and forced them behind her. Then, holding both her wrists in on hand he pushed her roughly against the wall and pinned her struggling body with his body. Once her anger had given way to fatigue much to the extent of collapse, she disintegrated into piteous sobs. She pressed her face into his chest. Mahesh could feel her shaking uncontrollably, her sobs raking her body. Mahesh felt her warm breasts pressed against his thudding heart, as if burning his skin.

Seeing his wife in such an absolute state of vulnerability made him believe that he had been too rushed into judging her. After a while, when the sobs had dissolved into snotty hiccoughs, Mahesh put his hand on her head and combed her hair with his fingers to cover the shorn area, lingering a little more than required. He could feel his wife lean completely onto him. He realized that it was the first time since his marriage that he had actually held her this close, and not have her removing his clothes in a rush. Her heart thudded against his chest at a very slow rate. None of the fiery, nymphomaniac urgency was there in the spent woman held prisoner in his arms.

He released her hands, her broken bangles made their way to the floor with some noise, but she did not move. He stepped away and still, she stood where she was, defeated. Mahesh was surprised by the blood covering his hands and he started to look for the source of the bleed. He realized that it was not his blood and he pulled out Uma's hands from her back and surveyed her wounds. Small punctures had bled profusely before shutting off. Mahesh was suddenly overcome with such tenderness for Uma that it took him by surprise. He walked his young and insecure wife to the bed where she sat down and drew her knees to her chest. Mahesh cleaned her wounds with clean water and managed to wrap them clumsily with a roll of bandage.

Then, he shifted his body and coaxed her to lie down. She did not protest; and like a child, she curled up on her side of the bed. Mahesh put his arm under her head as a pillow and she held his forearm with both her hands. Without saying anything, Mahesh turned his whole body towards her and matched his contour with hers. He threw his right arm over her and thereby cocooned her completely in his embrace. Soon, he felt her body sag into his. A steady rise and fall of her chest told him that she had fallen asleep. He buried his face into her hair and was himself lulled into a serene sleep. There, on the rickety bed, which was too fragile for the newlyweds, they found their symbol of stability and easy love, which came with understanding and communication. Mahesh was happy that he could touch his wife without lust. He was happy, that he finally loved....

CHAPTER TWELVE

Staying Afloat

The factory was the second most famous building in the village, after the Lord's house. Like two sturdy bookmarks, the two well-constructed concrete contraptions seemed to hold the rambling shambles of huts and shanties of the fishermen between them. Situated on the two extremes of the stretch of civilization, they had become famous locales. Each house was either right of 'the factory' or left of 'The Lord's house'. While the latter was an extravagance, with it's three floors and gold glided barristers and marble flooring, the 'factory' was more of a practical building. It was a singled floored building with four wings. Connected by dissecting hallways the four wings had their individual use and house management. Each wing was assigned separated responsibilities.

Keva Bai had employed only the local women in her factory, except for a couple of college going girls to manage the online sales and customer care department. The administrative and management work was handled by Keva Bai herself, and she was very territorial about it.

In the center of the factory, there was a display which was full of pictures of prominent authorities felicitating with Keva Bai. Several awards and certificates were framed and strategically placed in glass cases. But the place of highest honor was reserved for six portraits. The first one was that of Laxman Rao Bapat, the late husband of Keva Bai. The next two were those of his younger brothers Kirit and Suketu

Bapat. And the last two were that of Keva Bai's sons Keshav and Bhima Bapat. And there was one more picture of a young girl laughing, and it was obvious that the picture had been taken impromptu. It was neither garlanded, nor was there any incense burning in front of it. Rest of the portraits was garlanded with roses made out of sandalwood. A lamp was lit in front of the pictures, without fail.

It was a sort of ritual to pay homage to the departed souls, by touching the altar, before starting a new day. Keva Bai herself would do the same, before entering her office, whenever she was in the town. Somehow, the laughing girl stayed untouched… unseen… un-caressed. While staying in one of her palatial bungalows in the city, she visited the factory regularly, once every week. However, in her absence, one of the two young college girls managed the place on her behalf.

There was frenzy whenever Keva Bai was supposed to be around at the establishment. Everything was dusted, cleaned, arranged and re-arranged to perfection. The local employees would stand near the factory windows cramped up on each one trying to catch a glimpse of the elusive woman. Those who had seen her couple of times described her as a feisty woman of fifty with dark luscious hair tied in a tight knot behind her neck. A strip of white added to her aristocratic look. Her sharp and intelligent eyes were rimmed with fierce looking glasses. She was always seen in either a white or pale cream silk saree. A pair of diamond studs was the only jewelry she allowed on her body. A yellow spot of sandalwood adorned her forehead and her hair was always parted at the middle, empty, to signify that she was still in mourning for the loss of all of her family members.

Whenever she came to the factory, she visited the portraits swiftly, hardly laying eyes on them. It seemed more like a per functionary effort from her side. But if anyone had cared to see her when she thought she was alone and there was no one watching, they could not have missed the pain which radiated from her heart. Looking at them was as painful as it had been some years back. All the events of that fateful day came rushing in her mind whenever she dared to look into the eyes of the dead; questions without answers started to plague Keva

Bai. Could it have been avoided? Was there nothing that could have been done? Why had her sons decided to come back from London, that particular summer? Why had the brothers tried to kill her? Questions only the past could answer.

****

This was foolish. He was not in a television series. He was a doctor, sitting in an abandoned hut, located in the middle of nowhere. Sagar had not thought through the whole thing before making a dash for the wild. In his mind, it had made great sense in calling Revathi and asking for help. He had not taken into account things what might happen. He had no plan B. He was frightened. He was hungry and he was unsure of the depth of the muck pit he had pulled himself into. The unwanted visitor had made it very clear that he was something that needed to be taken care of.

After another day of wandering deeper and deeper into the jungle, he had stumbled upon a rumbling block of bricks with a tin roof. The place reeked of urine and feces. Sagar was sure that the view would be much more delightful in the morning. He had made his way to the cleanest place he could find and sat down on his haunches. Frustration and a sudden feeling of helplessness overwhelmed him. Where was he to go? What about his future? What about money? All he had was a few notes in his pocket which weren't enough for a ticket. He was without his phone or his trusted bike.

He knew that there was not a single person in the world who knew exactly where he was; and that including him who had lost track of location. That though soothed and agitated him with equal measures. Sure, there were no parents to mourn his loss, neither was there a wife or girlfriend. So while he would not be missed… he would not be missed? Sagar knew that after a certain time, his position will be filled in by the next in life. He will be eventually hunted down, and buried right where he will be killed, and no one will be the wiser. Unless… unless… Sagar suddenly stood up, his calves dehydrated and tired, knotting up in painful cramps. There was only one way out of this nightmare, and it was through it.

Dr. Sagar checked his luminous watch. It was a little over 2 am in the morning. There was utter silence and absolute darkness all around him. He had no way of judging the direction. He looked at the brightly lit sky and located the Jupiter. Although he had read about the star, he had no idea how he could use it to navigate. And even if he knew, how would he know the way? He had no idea where he was at that moment. All he knew was that he had to move fast, if he had to survive. It was a long shot, but he was not juggling with many options. His body screamed with the strain of unaccustomed previous running and trekking, but he knew that he had a little over 6 hours to get his plan working.

The plan was so fragile and immature. He debated whether the plan was worth risking his life for in the darkness, and perhaps getting bit by venomous animals, or mauled to death by the nocturnal jaguar. With his past experience, he knew that the jungle was replete with vipers. Every other day in the Health Center, he would be treating a couple of snake bites, bandaging lacerations, plastering broken bones and patching up stabbings…. He knew that he had more chances of surviving a snake's poison than the goons who were in search for him.

He thought about the body of the woman he had autopsied the day before… seemed like ages ago. How long, before he would be lying on the table himself? He suppressed a mirthless laugh.

His chances of lying on that table increases with time lost. He determined he was going to escape... he was never going to be found. How many graves were there in this jungle? Was he standing on one? The whole area belonged to them. The jungle, although an unknown terrain for him, was like the back of the hands of these assassins.

He knew that waiting in one place was reducing his chances of living to see the sun. He urged his legs to walk. Blood stagnated in his dilated veins and refused to rush back to his head. His shoes felt tight and his nylon socks dug deep into his shins. Still, he edged on, following the light of the brightest star in the sky, hoping and praying that his rudimentary knowledge of astrochemistry would lead him nearer to where he wished to be.

****

The bottles felt like small stones weighing down on his back. Every time someone called out to him, Ratan would stiffen and stop doing whatever he was doing. Since he had discovered such a large batch of cocaine in his house, he had not known what to do. He could not approach the police. Most of the police officers were criminals themself, and everyone knew on which side of the law they actually served. He could not go to the Lord; as he was sure that his Phooli had got this stash from him. What otherwise could explain the presence of this drug at his place? She had recently started visiting the Lord; and going by the timeline, Ratan could pinpoint exactly when, he started seeing the changes in his wife.

There was only one person he could go to. He had tied all the bottles in the plastic bag in which he had discovered them. Then he bound the bundle again with several layers of cloth and placed it inside his duffle bag and covered it with his clothes. He waited in his house, not daring to sleep, keeping his eyes on the horizon. Just as the sky lit up with the hues of orange and purple, Ratan, picked up the bag and left his house. As he made his way to the bus stand, he did not notice a certain man walking behind him.

Had Ratan cared to look at anything other than the horizon, he would have seen this person standing outside his house. The man, with his eyes on the quarry had picked up the sudden change of the tempo in the bereaved husband's behavior that there was no doubt in his mind, that the goods had been discovered.

Ratan Macchi, with one hand over his bag, and the other wiping the sweat running profusely down his face and neck, was making haste to get into the first bus which left for the city. The bus driver had already started the ignition and put the bus on first gear when a flustered

Ratan waved his hands to ask the driver to wait for him. Once the irate driver had thrown specific swear words at him, he stopped the bus long enough for him to get in. As the next person soon followed, the driver lashed out at him as well.

Ratan took an empty seat and tried to catch his breath. He did not notice the man get in the seat just behind him. He was still clutching his duffel bag with his right arm, resting it on the seat beside him. After some time, the conductor, who knew Ratan on a first name basis, came up to him to make small talk. He expressed his condolences at his recent loss, and admitted his surprise that he was travelling already. Ratan tried to be civil and calm. Then the conductor asked him where he wanted to go, and gave him a ticket with his change, and moved on after patting him awkwardly on his shoulder.

The man sitting behind was a little taken back. He had been waiting to follow Ratan to whichever place he was going to. But when he heard the name of the place, he was surprised. What was that phrase about a goat walking up to the slaughter-house himself? The man relaxed and stretched out his legs and used the hard wrought iron frame of the seat as a pillow. They were bound for the same destination. Ratan was not going anywhere. There were two hours to kill before they reached their destination. The man's relief lulled him into sleep. Waiting for the goat seemed to be much more tiring than killing it.

✳✳✳✳✳✳✳✳✳✳✳✳✳

Uma had woken up the next morning with Mahesh's arms around her, her head lying on his chest and the red vermilion having made crazy patterns on his white vest. Just as she moved, Mahesh woke up as well; the early morning rays of the sun were seeping in the room breaking into several threads of gold while passing through the seeming-magical mesh of Uma's hair. The clump of chopped hair was looking bizarre and childish. His otherwise well-kempt and beautiful wife had dark pools of sooth collected around her eyes where she had rubbed them with her fists. The sun was on her face and smeared all over her forehead. The lips were raw where she had bitten herself to keep herself from crying.

Mahesh got up and shifted his weight on his left elbow, while his head rested on his palm. He looked at his wife, framed against the brilliant new sun; her dusky skin glowing like freshly made sandalwood paste, her large eyes looking more exotic than ever, rimmed with the remnants of yesterday's kohl. When she did not make a move to go away from him, Mahesh dared to touch her left cheek with the flat of his palm. Her skin felt like churned out butter. Mahesh felt a thrill as he had never experienced before. It was like he had been having a feat with his eyes closed and hands tied behind him. Now, suddenly the blindfold was removed and he was allowed to see. And he was amazed with what he saw. He saw a little girl, just past her adolescence, stepping abruptly into the life of a woman, enchanted and frightened just as much as he was, sitting beside him.

Uma leaned her head towards his hand and nested it against her shoulder. Her cropped bangs fell over her right eye, but she did not seem to notice. Mahesh sat up and brushed her hair away. She seemed to stir herself wherever he touched her. Like a touch-me-not, every part he touched seemed to close and then open up again almost immediately, as if eager to be felt again. Mahesh complied. He watched as his wife blushed and blanched at the slightest of his touches. He cupped her face in his hands and drew her closer. Her eyes were closed. This time, it seemed she was too shy to look into his eyes.

Mahesh, moved by the strong feeling growing in his heart, kissed her closed eyes and the tip of her nose. He lingered his lips everywhere on her face, but kept her lips untouched. He trailed small kisses all along her long supple neck, ending just at the hollow at the end.

Uma was so taken in by his touch, that she had caught hold of his arms unknowingly urging her body towards him. Mahesh pulled away slowly and watched as his eager wife, her lips parted and red with desire, her body quivering with the anticipation of touch, her eyes, closed as not to reveal the truth in them… holding him in an embrace which had never felt so passionate, even when they had made love earlier. Every fiber of her body was charged and rustled with the energy of the feminine. Mahesh removed her clasped hands from his arms, momentarily breaking the charm, forcing Uma to open her eyes.

Mahesh was not smiling anymore. He was breathing heavily. And nothing could cover up the roaring of blood rushing throw his body with a feeling quite unmatchable than whatever he had experienced earlier. He took her small hands and placed them on his chest.

Several weeks earlier, Uma had made him feel her unbridled desire bursting from behind her breasts… but today; it was his turn to show his wife the difference between love and lust; and that at the epitome of both, neither are differentiable. He went on and touched her whole body first with his fingers and then with his lips, stopping her from coming any closer than required for him to map her body. Uma closed her eyes again, her body seemed to be burning with cold fire. Wherever he touched, he left a print, as if he had singled it with the tip of a burning piece of coal. His fingers, grazing lightly on her hardened nipples hidden behind the confines of her clothes, hurt as if he had slapped them.

Several times, she had tried to remove her hands from his chest and touch his manhood, just to assure herself of his arousal, but Mahesh refused to be touched. He was the doer today. This was his turn to show his wife that there were different ways to love. He insisted she kept her hands where they were, while he grazed her buttery skin beneath her saree. The short saree, unlike the 9 yards worn by most women, was hitched up from her ankles.

Mahesh had touched her previously, but now, in this moment, with his young bride bathed in the rays of the juvenile sun, he seemed to feel that he had never seen this woman before. He proceeded to remove each part of her clothing and keeping it aside neatly, followed by his own.

The slowness, and the restrain of not being allowed to move her hands, was maddening for Uma. Mahesh himself wasn't far away; his member, unaccustomed to having to wait for so long, was growing redder and angrier. The tip of his penis was pulsating and was growing almost purple with the blood stagnating in it… but Mahesh wouldn't stop today. He was setting the pace for all future encounters. He was going to have his wife as slowly and with as much reverence that her beauty demanded.

Today, it was not sex, but it was worship. He had decided to pay his homage to this exquisite woman who had danced into his life. It was a pleasure to see her red nipples standing up, the light brown areola puckered into the shape of a mouthful of jaggery. Her lower abdomen was shivering, trying to contain the uterus which had started to con-tract and relax at a maddening speed. Mahesh pulled her slowly so that they both were facing each other, sitting on their knees. Mahesh knew what he would find in between her legs. But he was surprised as his fingers touched moist lips dripping like honey oozing out of an over-loaded ripe beehive. He touched her and dared to feel deep within her, making her shout out to him to stop. Mahesh pulled back again, daring his wife to touch him, but the rising color of her neck and cheeks said a different story.

No longer could the Aphrodite look into her man's eyes. She could just surrender as he took control of her whole being and decided that she had been punished enough, by making her lie down, her head against the headrest. Then, with her hands held behind her head, Ma-hesh entered her welcoming vagina on his own will, without being guided or blinded by lust. He loved the woman lying under him. He was loving her, showing her that she mattered to him more than any-one else. This was his way of telling her, that she was his, just as she had made it clear on the first night that he was hers. Today, as the world welcomed a new day, this young couple discovered the magic of love and being loved… each as exotic and unique as the other.

CHAPTER THIRTEEN

The Fight for Life

Revathi massaged her temples. What had Sagar dragged her into? Once she had gotten to the safe house, she had switched on her phone. Immediately, a mail opened up on her screen. She entered the meaningless string of characters and she was overwhelmed by the large amount of data made being provided. She downloaded all of it in a pen drive. She knew that she had less than five minutes before anyone could trace her phone. She debated whether she should call her mother to tell her that she should not expect her any time soon. But then, she thought better of it. There was no use of winding her poor old mother into the drama. She was sure, her mother would understand either way… whether she alive or dead.

When she had taken up journalism as a profession, her mother had known that one day her daughter would invariably follow her late father's trails. He was a high end investigative journalist himself, who had come way too close to the truth. The drug mafia flourishing in the deeper veins of this picturesque tourist center, filled with innocent fishermen, had been a safe haven for drug peddlers for decades. The law had tried to curb them but always ended up scratching the mere surface; and largely turning a blind eye to the poisonous gangrene underneath which was eating up the country slowly but steadily. So defeated was the system by the powerful mafias that they had no other way out, other than become players of the same game.

Revathi's father had infiltrated so deep into the layers of the mastermind's world, that he was just about to expose the whole kingdom, when he was killed in a car accident. Revathi was but fifteen, when her mother had to go to the morgue to identify her dead husband by his birthmark on the right hand, the only part that could be picked out intact from the rest of the mangled mince. She had seen her mother shed a few silent tears in the station. She remembered how her mother had held her hand and walked her home; her gait sure and measured. Never once did she swoon and fall, never did she beat her chest to cry… she contained it, bottled it up in some part of her brain; where she kept her brave husband's memories.

Some weak moments, Revathi would find her mother sitting on the threshold of the veranda, one end of her pallu closed around her eyes and mouth, to stifle the sound of her sobs. So, when she had told her mother, with some reserve, that she wanted to pursue journalism as well, her mother had neither denied nor encouraged her. It was as if she always knew that this was inevitable. She only blessed her daughter every day and prayed to God that she may return back home at the end of each day.

The timer was set to go off at four minutes and thirty seconds, giving Revathi enough time to wind up whatever she was doing, switch off the phone, and dismember it. However, she so engrossed was she in the material that had opened up in front of her that she forgot about it. When it finally went off, she quickly did the needful; destroying both hers and Sagar's phone. For good measure, she threw them in the river which was flowing under the bridge.

The abandoned, rusted van parked amidst other debris, was the safest place Revathi could be. A couple of years back, while in search of some evidence to a breaking news, she had discovered the place. The van, made invisible by its common rusted and ugly looks had also hidden her at danger points, and most recently when a hitman following her had come so close that she could smell the toddy and sweat on his skin; but he could not find her. The access to the place was through a small lane filled with squatters; with the colony of people changing every two months; and therefore, her hideout was more or less secure. She had named the place: 'Rusty'.

Revathi opened a bag of chips and brewed herself some coffee. Once assured that she had not left any breadcrumbs on her way to Rusty, she redirected her attention to her laptop. Before she switched it on, she had activated the jammers which would keep any prying eyes from discovering her while she worked. The file Sagar had sent her was a compilation of numerous photographs of autopsies with the serial number of the bodies, as they were, unnamed.

In the last two years that the doctor had come here, he had autopsied five corpses, including the last one, brought to him by the police. On each instance, the body had been accompanied by PI Gaurang. Dr. Sagar had started smelling something more putrid than the corpses, when the policeman's visits became more regular and consistent. All the bodies discovered were that of women. None of them had been identified, and each had their fingers chopped off. A little dig into the past autopsies preceding his arrival brought up some similar cases. All the autopsies were either superficial or fabricated. There was nothing surprising that none were verified and signed by the late doctor.

Revathi opened each file and compared the findings. There was no doubt that somebody had been on a killing spree, targeting young women from poor socioeconomic backgrounds. But the last one stood out. She had been way too differently dressed. The choice of the saree and the combination of the bangles on her wrists told a story of a woman with a good sense of style. The red and yellow saree she had been draped in was pure silk. The toe rings were that of gold ...and she was pregnant.

Revathi mused… had this last one been murdered because of the child? Could it be just a copycat at work? If it was a copycat, then that meant the murderer of this particular woman knew about the previous other killings. It was possible then that the woman had been murdered by someone who had seen the chopped fingers… either the doctor, or….

****

The North Star had disappeared. The nice shady tree and a pitcher full of cool fresh water was so welcoming…. Dr. Sagar collected himself and dragged to the tree which seemed to go further and further. Delirious with fatigue and dehydration, he had started hallucinating. The scene in front of his eyes was going in and out of focus. And that was it? His tired mind slowly trying to be articulate. Is this how he was going to die? He could have just gone to his house that night. At least, his body would have been discovered. Now, in middle of nowhere, he would take less than a week to disintegrate into bones beyond recognition.

Sagar slumped. He turned and lay on his back, the sun blazing right on his face. But the heat had suddenly become bearable… rather cool. He was enjoying the feeling of the sun tickling his skin. It was extremely comfortable to lie there… he was sleepy. He deserved sleep…. Sagar decided to let his mind drift off for just a bit.

****

The ebb had drawn up the sea to its womb leaving the land beneath it strangely exposed, and vulnerable. If she had a life of her own, she would have blushed, her private life covered underneath the sea, like the face of a newlywed, brought out under the prying eyes of the human. But there was nothing the sea could do. She had to go when called as if rushing to meet a long lost lover. It had to be so, because whenever she came back, she was so exhilarated, so jubilant that it was only possible that her lover had kissed her. The tide felt like flush of ecstasy as if the sea had abandoned herself to the touch of her beau. But now it was the ebb.

The debris of a colony flourishing along its coast, lay bare and vulgar. Carcasses of dumped animals, plastic and loops of discarded fishing nets painted a gory picture. The natural habitants of the shells and the corals had been suffocated, banished from their own kingdom by this sea of human filth. Not only was the ebb unpalatable to look at, it was also associated with a nauseous stench when the barrage of garbage was subjected to the unforgiving sun.

The locals, having grown up alongside the sea had decided to not look in the direction of the sea when the ebb was there. They were afraid to see what lay beneath the serene looking sea. It was all good till the sea uncovered their misdoings. The reproach of the bare rash truth of the naked seabed was way too much for them.

But something must have made the random passerby look at the sea bed. His eyes met nothing new. He decided to look over the legs of the dead cows and dogs, sticking out of their bloated bodies, out towards the sky. He refused to register the muck of non-degradable plastic stuck inside the crevices of the rocks, painting the bare sea bed in a paradox of vibrant colors. The passerby urged the sea to come back. He urged her to cover up for their foolishness just one more time.

He shaded his eyes to look at the horizon to gauze the time when the tide will return. It was important for him, because he had to pick up the time carefully, so that he could bring the tourists to the 'beautiful' beach and tempt them to pose for at least a dozen photographs. That meant an average of 500 rupees from each over enthusiastic 'gora'. But the sea seemed reluctant to return anytime soon. It was well past 3 pm. The passer-by decided to return to the town. He walked a little before he stopped; and squinted his eyes again at the rocks. Something had caught his eye.

A glimmer of white… could have been the sea foam. He looked again, this time his pace accelerating towards the speck of white. He rushed to the man lying on his stomach, his face buried in the sand. The degree of moisture in his shirt suggested that he had been in the sun for about an hour. Gingerly the man toed the body with his bare feet. He felt warm… could be because of the sun? But then, the 'body' took in a rasping breath and chocked on the sand. The passer-by was surprised. It was very rare for the sea to spit out a living being. If she had, then it must be the sign of God for him.

The man turned the gasping man over and pulled out as much as he could from his nose and mouth. The body moved and opened its eyes slowly, temporarily blinded by the sun. The passer-by fished out his phone and fumbled to dial the number of the ambulance. Had he been standing nearer he could have heard the words spoken by the drenched and drowning man.

"Kasturi..." was all the doctor managed to say before the world became a dark and silent place.

CHAPTER FOURTEEN

Duty to Self

The man must have been waiting for his chance. He must have known all along, where he was off to. he must have taken a seat and placed himself at a vantage point. What had he planned? Had he planned to slip the thin wire around his neck when the bus lurched? How sure was he that the man intend to harm him? After all, what did he know? Did he have any proof? Except for the occasions on which he had caught him staring at him in the rear view mirror. For the most part of the journey, the man had been asleep. It was only at the beginning of the steep ride up the mountain that the man had woken up.

After that he had neither moved nor looked at his direction. Several times, Ratan had tried to catch him looking at him again. But it never happened. Finally, he had relaxed. It was probably all a work of his pumped up imagination. He had allowed himself to take a few winks himself. The snaking road was making the passengers sway in its vogue; the rash driving of the driver was not helping either. Several times, the bus jumped over invisible bumps and potholes.

The jarring sensation down the spine was probably due to the bumpy ride, thought Ratan, when a sharp pain seared through his body through his left lumbar area. It was only after he had turned to check the moisture on his shirt, had he realized that he was bleeding. Automatically, his eyes were drawn towards the image of his co-passenger. Not only was he looking at him, he was watching him die. Ratan must have misjudged his own strength when he had turned around abruptly with the intension of pushing him away. The bus decided to lurch at the same moment and Ratan's left elbow shot directly into the man's windpipe. He did not even wince or grunt, but just slumped over, a small sharp pocket knife clanging on the floor, haven slipped out of his hand.

The man looked surprised and his face held on the look even posthumously. Ratan had almost shouted out to the driver to stop the bus. But then, once the onus of the act dawned upon him, he sat down again. The pain on his back was ebbing into a dull thud. An acute urge of urination came over him. He covered his red stained shirt with a sweater and motioned to the conductor to stop the bus. When none of the duo showed any inclination to do so, Ratan dashed out of the bus with his duffle bag, as it slowed down at a corner to take a precarious turn. His bursting bladder was threatening to void on its own account.

Somehow he maneuvered his way in the reckless bus and steadied his shaking body by bracing on the barricade. Without any further ado, he released his penis and waited for the urine to come. A sharp pain shot down in his left side of the groin from the lumbers, but not a drop of urine came out. He panicked… the pain overwhelming and pushing him to the verge of collapsing. Then suddenly as the pain had come, it disappeared with the appearance of the first drops of urine. Glad that his ordeal was finally over, he looked down. A thin stream of blood was flowing in between his feet, punctuated by long threads of clots. The blood thinned into a clearer stream midway and fortunately, ended with a clear flow.

Ratan knew that he had been stabbed in his left kidney. He stood up and started to think back at whatever had happened in the last few hours. His thoughts were cut short, as the feeling of a full bladder told him that he was bleeding continuously. He needed to find help… and quickly.

Charu looked at the naked inspector, stroking his oddly bald looking member. He was standing with his feet apart, a smirk on his face, and the crazy look he always had in his eyes. She had agreed to see him tonight, partly because she did not intend to hear him whine anymore, and partly because she had sensed a tinge of menace in his voice. She was smart enough to know when it was too much. She loved peddling her men on, bringing them on the verge of madness with desire. In her experience, these kind of men performed the best.

It was way too easy to challenge their egos... to stroke it, literally; titillating and tantalizing by refusing them pleasure of any sort. Most of them, unable to contain themselves, often found recluse in the battered bodies of their wives or other less experience whores. But Charu wanted the best. She deserved the best, because that is what she gave them.

Initially, fresh into the trade, she had always felt like a wife. Obligated to spread her legs and close them when the man was done. Her satisfaction was never a part of the equation. Soon, she realized that getting turned on and climaxing for real made the men happier and come back for more. The surety and validation of potency that her moans and the torrent of wetness dripping between her legs brought to men, made them come back for more. It was not her sex appeal or the ampleness of her breasts and buttocks which lured them. She was sure that most of her customers had fuller and prettier wives at home. The men came to her hungry for her total abandon… her hero worship.

The penis looked like some obscene pink umbrella in the PI's hand as he rubbed it, trying to bring it to life. Occasionally he threw a glance at her direction to see if she was laughing at him.

Once or twice he had committed the mistake of pulling her head towards his groin; she had playfully slapped his testicles and squeezed them with a little bit of extra force. Charu knew better than to laugh at him. His service pistol was hanging from his belt, close to hand. She knew what he could do with his bare hands.

Often, while having sex with her, he had rattled on about the way he had raped his wife over and over again. Something about the pain and plight of the hapless woman seemed to arouse him. Sometimes, he would try and choke her as well. She had not complained initially. Then one day, with his penis in her mouth, he had shoved himself further in. Charu had jerked her head back, in the process biting the base of the engorged penis. He had sprung back like a cat on coals, his dick held between his thighs, screaming and crying in pain. Although she had smoothened things later by more than compensating for the accident, she knew, that she had an infallible weapon up her sleeves. She knew what she would do the next time he forgot to clearly differentiate between her and his wife.

The shaved groin made him look like an oversized baby. His unresponsive phallus wasn't helping either. She was getting bored. Yawning was as bad as laughing. She stifled her yawn converting into a wink and lick of her lips. The PI, encouraged by the come hither was immediately much more confident. His organ seemed to be responding as well. Charu waited mechanically and impassively for the straddle, for the push and the relentless thrusts. She closed her eyes and thought about a particular person. This had helped her sail through the nonstop flow of men and their sweaty, lust ridden bodies thrashing into her.

The face she imagined had kissed her heart... literally. Once, when he had touched her, she had felt her heart skipping the fabled beat, for the first time since she was but twenty. He had not asked for sexual favors, nor had he made a move. He had simply come and converted her into a flower in bloom. Charu, fancied herself in love. She was a practical whore. She neither wished nor dreamt of a family or house. She was happy with her youth and had planned to enjoy it while it lasted. But the man just made it easier to feel as if it was all real. Most of the times she actually climaxed as the face filled up her mind. She was lucky that she was not in the habit of shouting out names....

＊＊＊＊＊＊＊＊＊＊＊＊＊

The bus braked suddenly, bringing it to a halt. The travelers were shaken out of their reprieve. The driver grinned sadistically at the reflection of the people shaken out of their sleep unceremoniously. Feeling successful, because that had been his exact intension, he jumped off his seat, before the mandatory angry grumbles from the people could mar his mood. For all he could care, they could all fall in the ditch and meet their maker. That is, all, except him. He yelled at the conductor who followed suit ignoring the passengers haggling for their measly change. Waving them off, promising to make up in the next trip, the conductor joined his partner going for a second breakfast.

A cursory glance convinced him that no one was lingering in the back seat with mischief in their minds, no suspicious creaks… no unclaimed luggage. More than once, he had discovered school going children making out in the back seat. He was good to go. He stepped out of the bus, slamming the door with a resounding thud.

The empty bus was still full of the residuals of rancid breaths and sweat. The sun, beating down on its roof was doing nothing to make it any better. On certain days, an unlucky passenger or two would be left sitting in the oppressing heat, waiting for the driver to finish his tiffin so they could continue their journey to the next town. Fortunately today, there was no living being left to stew in his perspiration.

The omnipresent flies were buzzing around trying to find fodder. A large cloud of flies seemed to have located a treasure trove of food. Somebody must have left some form of undigested or partially digested food on the seat. But there was no one to check. Had the conductor paid attention, he would have realized that one of his passengers had not aligned. If he had taken the trouble of walking up the corridor, he would have seen the passenger slumped on his side, his eyes partially open and the flies making a mad rush to the most easily accessible and edible part… the inside of the mouth. The dark moist place ideal for laying eggs appealed to the flies which roared and made a dash for it. They needed not hurry. They had lots of time.

CHAPTER FIFTEEN

Revealing the Nuts

The Lord was looking at the small stack placed on the table in front of him. He knew these were the passports of the thirty females who were bound for Nepal in the coming month. The girls had to be changed on a regular frequency to create chaos and absence of any pattern. Each girl had been selected randomly from all across the country. Each had a life span of four and sometimes, if lucky, five trips. After a maximum of five immigration stamps, neither the passport nor the girl was ever seen again.

The ingenious boss had always used a base for not more than three years. By the time the police got uncomfortably hot on their trails, the whole place would have been shut down, destroyed, and left to look like a barren land. The Lord's house had been in its third year. It was inevitable to go under the hammer soon. He had made this place his own and ruled here for more than a decade. The mere idea of losing it was like a physical blow to him. No amount of compensations, or promises of being included into the closest ring of the boss, felt alluring enough. He opened the drawer and took out the clipping which had been sent to him as a wrapping. More like a warning, he thought.

Many times he had thought about coming clean to the police, when the ghosts of his dead family haunted his dreams. But with time, the ghosts faded away. His past life dissolved in the present life's glory, power, and lust. How could anyone blame him? In his mind, everything that was happening was a part of God's ulterior motives for him. Had he asked to be a saint?

The people propelled him to the altar to appease their own guilt ridden minds. Like all mortals they needed someone to tell them that it was ok. Had he asked for the women to present themselves to him in full devotion and abandon? They wanted the touch of the mystical, which seemed to light them up. Who was he to say no to God's plans? In fact, he had been instrumental in easing the inevitable crossing over to the other world by loving them… bringing them closer to God than they had ever been? Women opted to have the last trip ending at his house. The serenity along with divine sex and cocaine, presented a heady concussion which eased their end. The less fortunate ones were either sent to the boss or one of the close associates.

The girls, once inside the ring, had no way of escaping alive. Over the years, the Lord had kept an outlook for the occasional bodies which had been washed up on the shore. In collaboration with the local police, the things were covered up with such ease and detachment, that the Lord felt that his heinous acts of the past looked tame in comparison.

He opened the stack tied together in brown paper with rubber bands. He went through each of the passports. Some of the girls he knew, some were new. For some, it was their fifth trip. And there was one passport which was not going to be needed anywhere. The Lord sighed. Would anyone understand if he told them about her? Was it entirely his fault that he had fallen in love with her? Had she nothing to do with it? Had it been he who had wooed and seduced her, or was it the other way? Will they agree with him that the innocence of a child was the most potent and fool proof technique of seduction?

She was not even supposed to be there. She wormed her way into his life out of her own sheer will. She had been one of the devotees, swaying and singing with the others and merging her soul in the house and its aura, as if they belonged to her.

A little thought gnawed at his mind, nevertheless. Every time he thought of her swaying dancing body, removing each part of clothing as she sang, he could not ignore the prick of 'bliss' he used to give. Everything had started when she was brought by her exceedingly stupid husband, thinking that he had the cure for everything. So enchanted was the Lord by this dusky supple skinned woman, that he had decided to make her his own… even if that meant for a day.

The husband had run away from the threshold itself. But the girl had a certain kind of courage which verged on the brink of stupidity. She had walked straight up to him and prostrated. The scant heave of her budding womanhood was full of promises. When asked to hold out her hand in order to show her trust, she had put forth both. In the ruckus of song, dance and heady fumes of frankincense, she did not even register the prick of the hypodermic needle. Her virgin body with the surge of dopamine could not contain the heat within. She had danced and removed all the pins from her head, her saree coming off as she tread on its pallu. The flimsy blouse, torn at several places became too much to bear. She bared not only her soul, but all of her that day.

The Lord, overcome with something other than lust had again seen this as a sign of atonement from God, giving him a second chance to make amends of sins done in the past. Later, when she came against her own will, she would be often forlorn and sad. She would sit at the far end of the assembly with her body collected and closed around her like a closed flower. Moreover, whenever the Lord came up to her, she will withdraw with a look of a hunted animal in her eyes. It was clear that she hadn't been able to gather enough courage to tell her husband anything about the first day of her visit.

The Lord, overcome with the fear of rejection compelled her to come to his chambers under some pretext or the other. She would come, with her head stooped low, almost disappearing in her torso. The Lord, knowing only too well how to comfort such wounded and scared women, mellowed her with songs praising God and the virtues of total abandon. The nitrous oxide mixed subtly in the air helped to ease the unprepared and the unwilling into a world, where all ideas seemed as if branching from their own subconscious. For the next few hours, the drugged and dazed victim became Meera, Radha, Mohini or Yamini... whatever the Lord wanted.

Slowly, she became addicted to the bliss and soon she stopped bothering about the source of the bliss. The Lord, started to experiment with her before receiving his own consignment of mules. In one of their erotic consumptions, she had seeded the small bottles filled with simple plain salt in a peach, and she had eaten it all on his command. He had proceeded with another peach.

Then he had seated his head on her right thigh, his mouth prying open her vagina. With each lick, as her vagina quivered and opened, he inserted pellet after pellet, until a small budge above her pubis suggested that she could probably hold no more. A nulliparous womb could hold only so many. The Lord, in his dry run, had finally concluded that a woman who was on an empty stomach, and had not born any children could hold as many as 150-200 such pellets. He was not bothered about the pellets he had inserted. He knew that she would pass them unnoticed. The ones in the womb were removed by a mid-wife in one of the drug induced stupors.

By the end of the month, so hung was she on the drug and the Lord that she craved for it, and was ready to exchange sex for drug. She was an ideal mule, trained, hitched and ready to do anything for a high. A mule was worth a lot of income. The Lord, once bored of the once feisty, lively woman, whose shell had remained back, decided to cut his losses by including her as one of the mules. The boss had been skeptical but had finally agreed.

It must have been a cursed day for the Lord, when he decided to give the stash of pellets to her with instruction for how to insert them in her body. He refrained from doing it himself, as the once fresh and pristine red vagina had turned a dirty shade of yellow and pumped out green discharge. That was the last day he had seen her. When she did not return the next day and then again, he was frightened for the first time. He had tried asking around subtly, but no one had been able to tell anything more than that she was extremely sick and bedridden. An irrational fear had gripped the Lord. What if she had ratted him out? Would she dare to do so? And what about the pellets? She had cocaine worth millions with her.

That day, when Phooli's husband had come searching for him, he had been alerted. To get some guidance, he had called the boss and could hear the disappointment at the other side. He had let the boss down. He knew that everything would be taken care of once the boss was in the picture. He was sad that Phooli had to see such an unnecessarily messy end. But his fear of being exposed or being at the other end of the room was bigger than his rudimentary affection for the woman. He watched as one of his henchmen left after receiving a call… one of the closest to the boss. His heart sunk for a notch before it soared at the sight of the people who had gathered at his veranda.

As he came down, he swept the crowd with his eyes, and located the husband. He had dealt with him in an off-handed manner. He had thought that it was the best approach. The disheartened husband, having found that the Lord was less than eager to even recognize him, had left like a fool does. But the recent events had convinced the Lord, that Ratan Macchi was not as stupid as he had taken him for.

A little research revealed that not only had he been well known to the world of drugs, but he had been a user in his teens. Now sober and on the way to a happy married life, he had lost all that he had ever cared for in his life. The trouble now was that the wounded man was missing and the man sent to finish him off had been found dead in the back seat of a bus. On a second thought, the Lord realized that he should have been more careful with the husband. Maybe he shouldn't have let him leave.

CHAPTER SIXTEEN

In the Den

Uma had carefully combed her hair to hide the evidence of the impulsive haircut. With buds of mogra and jasmine adorning her bun, and a bunch of red roses tucked behind her right ear, there was little to no evidence of the mishap. Dressed in a sea green silk saree and new slippers, she walked a step behind Mahesh, as he led the way to the factory.

The idea of working had little attraction for Uma. If anything, it irked her more to think that Mahesh was finding ways to keep her away from his plans of going to the deep sea. As soon as they crossed the small strip of the outland sea water, with the help of a dinghy, the factory rose above the small shanties surrounding it. Although a modest establishment as compared to few in the neighboring towns and cities, this was an awe inspiring building for the simple fishermen folks who lived there.

Uma, her pallu held tightly under her chin with her right hand, watched with wonder. The clean and meticulously kept gardens and turf grass were a sight in themselves. Beyond the lawn was a small pink colored fountain which was pouring out water from concealed faucets. The factory faced the fountain.

Uma and Mahesh removed their slippers outside the entrance and walked bare-footed into the office. Earlier, Mahesh's brother had spoken to someone in the office and fixed up an appointment for ten in the morning. The couple sat nervously at the edge of their chairs. The cool air from the air conditions and the pristine white walls filled them with apprehension.

For someone, who had never seen anything this beautiful and re-fined, such cleanliness and order, it was an uncomfortable situation. A glance at the wall clock showed that they were a full fifteen minutes early than the purported time. The white marble floor reflected the ceiling lights. Uma lifted off her feet from the floor, fearing that her dirty feet might stain it. And after waiting for five minutes, both of them were so agitated that they were convinced that coming here had been a foolish idea after all.

Just when they were about to make a dash for the door, a young girl, dressed in white, walked up the corridor, busy in conversation on the phone. Without breaking her stance, she looked at the highly strung couple and flashed a genial smile in their direction, immediately making them feel at home. With a motion of her free hand, she asked them to follow her into the office. With the help of her card, she opened the door as it pinged the green light of authorization. Mahesh and Uma watched on, fascinated at this bit of technology.

They meekly followed the girl inside an office which was decorated tastefully with a cushy big chair, a dark brown working table and two simpler yet elegant chairs in front of it. The walls were adorned with pictures of various people and important events. Far on the left corner was a kind of small bed or divan, covered in white leather. While the girl took her place in one of the simpler chairs, she pointed out the divan to them.

They walked over to the spotless piece of furniture and fidgeted, unsure of what they were supposed to do. Surely, she was not expect-ing them to sit on something so beautiful and exclusive! They walked over to the divan and after a minute of contemplation, they sat down on the floor, on their haunches. The girl, still on the phone engaged in a flow of intense conversation, crinkled her bows, and terminated the call.

She smiled at them and insisted that they sat on the divan. After much cajoling, they agreed. Mahesh was the first to get up, and Uma followed suit. Once all of them were seated, the girl asked the reason for their visit. When told, she nodded and fished out her phone again, made a call and confirmed that they were indeed expecting a new woman to join the factory. Mahesh, at a loss of words could just mumble. The girl was trying hard to make them comfortable but all her smiles and antics were only making them more tongue tied.

Finally, defeated, the girl walked over to Uma and placed a kind hand on her shoulder. In response, Uma shrunk in her oversized saree a little bit more. The girl offered them a tour of the place and a chance to see other women at work. Mahesh and Uma looked at each other and mutually agreed. They followed in haste behind the girl who was already out of the office and half way through the corridor.

They walked into a lift which magically transported them to the top floor which opened into an open area surrounded by glass walls. There, at least thirty women were bent over a huge stack of sea shells of all possible colors and shapes, their hands busy in aligning them carefully into decorative pieces. The girl motioned to a woman who, unlike others, was dressed in clothes similar to the girl and was not having her hands in the pile of sea exoskeletons. The other woman was also young, although much less prettier than the ever smiling one. A rapid exchange in English between them seemed to be about Uma. The less pretty one stole a glance or two at Uma as if measuring her up. After a half-hearted affirmative nod from her, Uma was shepherded to the place where the women were seated. A silence prevailed as the women looked up at their newest addition.

Uma was led to a small table at the farthest corner of the room and assigned to a woman almost her own age who was separating the sea shells according to their shapes and colors. With a vague instruction to 'watch', she was left alone with the sorter who looked at her and smiled. Uma looked back to locate Mahesh, but he was nowhere to be seen. In spite of the warm welcoming smile of her first acquaintance, Uma felt unnaturally uncomfortable and edgy.

Meanwhile, just as Uma had turned the corner, the girl with the bright smile had held Mahesh's hand, much to his surprise, and walked him back to the lift. Once there, she introduced herself as Meera, the Manager of the factory. She stopped at each level of the establishment and showed him around. The grand tour was uncalled for, thought Mahesh, whose mind was still with Uma and the feeling of unease he had felt. As much as he tried, he couldn't shove off the feeling.

Once back in the office, Meera took out a form and entered Uma's details and asked him to sign at the bottom. Again, unsure and afraid of sounding naïve and stupid, Mahesh did not question the print on the paper. He signed it and stood up immediately. Folding his hands in a Namaste, he asked her when he should come back to collect his wife. The woman seemed to smile a little brighter and answered that he need not bother about that. When he did not make any move, the woman's smile faltered a little. With an edge creeping up in the friendly tone, she repeated her answer and added that Uma will be transported back to his house by the company-owned bus.

Mahesh, still with his hands folded in front of the chest, bowed to her, and walked out of the office, and out of the main door of the factory; he took several deep breaths and put on his sandals. Uma's slippers, arranged neatly beside his own, looked very small and child-like in comparison to his. Mahesh was overcome by an extreme feeling of longing to see his wife. He felt guilty of having been the one to have insisted on her taking up employment in the factory.

He picked up the dainty looking slippers and placed them neatly back again beside a pot of extraordinarily brilliant green plant. Mahesh noticed that the plant was artificial as was the grass laid out on the lawn.

The place, grand as it seemed, was wrapped up into plastic. Every-thing about it gave a vibe of being assembled in haste, and artificial, like the girl's fake buoyancy. As he made his way out, Mahesh tried to put his finger on that particular thing, which had made him feel uncomfortable. Was it the white walls? Was it the access card? Had it something to do with the women working on the third floor, or the several mysteriously-looking locked rooms on the second floor?

As he climbed the dinghy heading back to his part of the village, an irrational fear gripped his heart. As the dinghy chugged its way across the backwater, the island with the fake cheerful building became smaller and smaller, until all Mahesh could see was the grey blue water of the sea.

****

Revathi looked at the picture. The small vials were familiar. For someone who had grown up in the world of crime and drugs, the 1x1 pellet was a common sight. She knew, she was looking at the partial remains of the container used to transport cocaine across borders. In all probability Dr Sagar had come across these by chance and it had taken him four more bodies to confirm his theory. In the detailed autopsy report which he had entered against each body, he had concluded that the women had been strangled to death and later their digits chopped off meticulously to avoid any chance of identification. They had been probably thrown deep in the sea to abolish the chances of their discovery. Maybe the murderers had become way too lazy or callous and had stopped taking the pain to go far into the sea.

Revathi knew that there was a thriving business of drug peddling right under her nose. For years, she had been trying to gather evidence against the mastermind, called as simply 'the boss'. Without any personal information or even a photograph of the elusive 'boss' it was almost impossible to write up a convincing story. Her numerous attempts to have her theory printed in the newspaper had been subject to ridicule. In a way, Revathi agreed with her editor. They could not publish a story just on a hunch. Now, she had landed herself a goldmine of information.

She went through the whole file again. That was when she found a file named 'the accident', which she had missed initially. She clicked on the icon. It was a large one and would require some time to download. Revathi slid the hot laptop off her lap and stretched her legs. The running and the treasure hunting had made her legs sore. She got up and boiled some water on a small gas stove. With a bag of her favorite strawberry-mango herbal tea dipped in the water she walked towards the laptop. The file had opened.

It was a cut out of a very old news. It was about an accident in which the vehicle, a seven-sitter car had allegedly lost control and fallen in the very ditch she was hiding at the moment. She sat down, her tea forgotten, as she read the news, which she knew all too well. Six people had died in the accident. Their bodies had been found in the car, buckled to their respective seats. Revathi reread the whole article. She could not understand why Sagar had included this particular piece in the file of evidence. For a very long time she kept on staring at the article. It did not make sense. She did not read out the names of those who had died. She knew them by heart. Her logical mind could not come up with any explanation. For the world of it, she couldn't understand what her father's death had to do with all this.

CHAPTER SEVENTEEN

It was Murder

Ratan Macchi stood in front of the toilet bowl. Three times in the last couple of hours, the water in the bowl had turned crimson red with the blood in his urine. This time, to his relief, the color was that of straw, with no evidence of blood in it. He had braved his way downhill on feet and taken shelter in one of the cheap lodgings. He had reasoned that going to a doctor for medical help would raise questions, and maybe the police would find out that he was in the same bus as that of the now dead assassin. His fear of getting caught overruled his health concerns.

Gradually, the pain had ebbed into a dull thud and his urine frequency had reduced. The blood from the stab had ceased long back. Now, the urine was also clear. Fatigued by fear, guilt, and loss of large amount of blood, Ratan's body was on the edge of collapse. He dragged himself out of the bathroom and threw himself on the mattress with questionable sanitary standards. The lumpy bed and the stained sheets were the least of his concerns. He had a long way to go. But for now, he needed to sleep.

****

Constable Tatya's index finger on the right hand had turned a brilliant shade of red. The nail had been pushed out of its bed and a yellow-black liquid had escaped from the nail bed. He had accidently crushed his finger in the door hinge. A makeshift bandage made out of a random lying cloth had stalked the blood but had infected the wound. The fact that he was diabetic and a toddy lover had made things worse. The pain was unbearable and Tatya could feel a fever forming itself somewhere around his solar plexus.

It was an unwritten rule in the police station, that under no circumstances were they allowed to visit the PHC to seek medical advice. If inevitable, the doctor in the city 60 km from the village was the first choice. So for the better part of the day, the constable had written reports and fielded call with his index finger raised up, trying not to let it get in the way. By afternoon the fever had reduced him to a shivering disoriented man. His colleagues, who knew about his illness thought it was better to break the rule just this one time and drove him to the PHC.

There they were met with a huge crowd of patients. They seemed agitated. Few of them were arguing with the ward boy who was waving them off like a swarm of flies. The arrival of the police jeep dispersed the crowd. The people knew that the police was bad news at any time of the day. The ward boy spit out a long trail of red beetle nut juice and walked towards the jeep, wiping his mouth with the back of his hand. The police constables in the jeep looked at the irate crowd and wanted to know the reason. The ward boy smirked and let out a laugh which sounded more like a cough. He told them that the doctor hadn't been seen for the past three days.

Tatya, burning with fever and excruciating pain in his finger was distressed; the spreading rubor in his hand all the way up to the forearm was not a good sign. The greenish yellow pus seeping through the dirty bandage wasn't good either. The ward boy craned his neck to have a better look at the back of the van, where Tatya was lying down, breathing heavily and unnaturally. The ward boy had seen a fair share of patients in his lifetime and knew from experience that the constable was in a very bad shape.

For a moment, he was genuinely concerned about the man. He

went back to the PHC and came out with the nurse, running on her short stout legs, trying to keep pace with the younger agile man. The back of the van was opened. The musky smell of an infected wound hit the old nurse and she recoiled a bit. She agreed that the constable was indeed ill and needed immediate care. The policemen decided to make a dash to the city but were informed that the only access road was under construction. The detour was a long one and would make the constable's condition worse.

By now, Tatya had slipped into an unconscious state. His eyes had rolled up and only the whites were visible. The nurse put her fingers on the sick man's wrist and felt the feeble pulse racing like a train. She knew that the man was very sick and, without some immediate action, he was bound to die. She told the policemen so, and offered to at least bridge over the present crisis with medicines available at the clinic. Tatya was carried by all four of his limbs. The legs were held by the two policemen who had accompanied him and the nurse and ward boy took hold of the hands.

The rotund constable was quite weighty. The four of them were unable to hoist him high enough. As a result, his opulent buttocks scraped over the gravel on the way to the clinic. His globular abdomen rolled from side to side like that of a bloated whale. It was a good thing that Tatya was unconscious. Otherwise, the people gathered around the clinic, just to have a look at the fallen policeman would have embarrassed him.

Once in, they heaved him with all their might and dropped him on one of the five beds, none of which had any mattress on them. The metal mesh of most of them had caved in with years of overuse. The mattresses had been destroyed by vermin long back and sheets or pillows were not to be even thought of. The nurse decided to waste no more time and deftly took an IV line on his good hand and started an infusion. A rapid blood analysis showed that the sugar had shot up sky high. Then she cut open the bandage with a small scissor. The length of cloth had stuck on the finger with the dried up pus and blood. The nurse tried to wet it with some saline to loosen it. When that failed, she just yanked it off the finger. An angry red line extending from the bulbous infected finger had crept all the way up to the middle of the forearm.

The nail had avulsed from the nail bed. The tip of the finger had turned into an unhealthy color of grey. The nurse shook her head sadly. This was way above her expertise. She cursed the missing doctor mentally, and at the same time prayed for his safe return. She cleaned the wound as best as she could and covered it with sterile dressing. She had very few antibiotics in her kitty, some of which were approaching their expiry date. She took a chance and gave him the medicines hoping for a miracle.

The angry policemen were demanding the whereabouts of the doctor and insisting on his presence. The hapless non-medical staff told them that they did not have the slightest idea and were themselves baffled. The ward boy had been to his house when he was unreachable on his cell phone. He had found the house locked and his bike missing. There was no immediate family who could throw any light on where the doctor could have gone.

The old nurse was worried, when she was told that the doctor was not at his house. The incidence a few years back, wherein the then medical officer had been found dead, seemed to be repeating itself. The nurse was very fond of the new young doctor, and had pampered him with occasional homemade food and delicacies. He was like the son she never had. The doctor, in return, loved and respected her. To be dealt with such professionalism and respect was something new for the old nurse and it only elevated the doctor high up in her mind.

When he did not turn up for the third day, she knew that something bad had happened to him. She had been in two minds about approaching the police for help. She knew that the present PI Gaurang was as corrupt as one could get. She also knew the particular disdain the PI had for the doctor; so, she had kept mute.

But today, the dynamics had changed. She decided to call the head office and report the doctor missing from duty. They would send a replacement, she was certain of that. Once the new doctor was in office, it would feel like a closure on the chapter of Dr. Sagar Hegde. The nurse looked at the cheap aluminum door of his OPD and the name stenciled on it with red tape. Soon, the tape would be removed and a new one fashioned to spell the name of the new doctor. Life would go on.

The nurse took out the thermometer she had placed under the unconscious constable's armpit. It read 104 degrees F. The nurse looked at the man, heaving unnaturally, his vein at the neck jumping erratically. She knew that if he did not get immediate medical attention, he would die in less than 48 hours.

There was some halfhearted discussion amongst the other constables regarding carrying him to another hospital situated a little more than 100kms from there. The rickety old jeep could not be trusted for the task. The only other option was the van, but the driver had gone to his own village, and was not expected back for at least the next two days. They decided amongst themselves to discuss the matter with their PI, and left their sick colleague in the clinic. By now, the patients had also left. The ward boy had slipped out long back.

The realization, that she might have to stay back the night, disappointed the nurse. She had been counting on Tatya's family member to stay the night. But apparently, there were none to call. Most of his family stayed in Nasik and it would take them at least one day to come to the village. The old nurse, fatigued and hungry after a long grueling day had to stay back, her sense of duty getting the better of her. She adjusted the fluids and other medicines and sat on a chair beside the sick man. Another temperature check showed that the fever was stubborn and was not coming down.

The nurse had known Tatya since he had been a strapping young man, newly recruited in the police force and full of fresh ideas and ideologies. Sadly, she had sadly seen him gradually disintegrate into just another stereotype Government employee who cared for nothing which happened after working hours.

The nurse decided that a cold sponge might help with the fever. She started applying wet pieces of bandages on his head. After an hour the fever seemed to have come down a notch. Tatya had regained some of his consciousness and was babbling incoherently in his stupor. Soon, he broke up in sweat and drenched his khaki uniform. A tentative hand on the forehead told the nurse that the worst part seemed to be over. Relieved, she threw back her head on the hard back of the chair and lifted her feet on another to rest them.

****

The breathing of the sick man had returned to a much normal rhythm. The nurse looked at his face, now blanched as the redness of fever ebbed away. She felt her eyelids drooping and she felt it was safe for her to catch some sleep herself, and in no time, she was asleep.

A loud bang shook her out of her slumber. For a few minutes, she could not register where she was exactly. Once she was a bit more oriented, she looked at the bed. Tatya was sitting up on the bare wrought iron bed trying to get to the jug of water kept on the table. In the process he had shoved off the medicine tray to the floor.

The nurse got up and helped him with some water. She called him out by his name to calm him. The dazed look in his eyes meant that he was confused and hadn't recognized her. He looked around and got agitated, trying to remove his bandages and the iv-drips. The nurse forced him back on the bed. Tatya looked at her with red shot eyes. She refused to be bullied by a patient, sick or not. She took out a vial from the medicine cabinet and pushed it into his vein. Slowly, he mellowed and the crazy look left his eyes. He was mumbling again and the nurse went closer to catch what he was saying. The three words he said confused the nurse yet some more.

"Kasturi was murdered."

The nurse was surprised at this revelation. What had Kasturi got to do with Constable Tatya? Everyone in the village knew when she died, and Tatya himself had accompanied her corpse to the hospital, a few months back.

She felt an uncomfortable chill in the middle of her back. It was not that Tatya was uttering the name of a long dead woman, which frightened the nurse. It was the classified knowledge that she had been murdered, which plagued her. She was the only person, other than the doctor, who knew about the autopsy report. For some reason unknown to her, the doctor had decided to change his findings in the report. She hadn't thought twice about it, and with only one year to go before her retirement, she did not want to stir the murky water and make it murkier.

But today, hearing the deranged man speak about murder had confirmed her suspicion. The police knew as clear as daylight that the woman had been murdered. And this could only mean that they were hand in glove with whosoever was the murderer. Out of the two people, asides the police, who knew the truth, one was missing and probably dead. The incidence of the suicide of the previous doctor clubbed with the new one missing was slowly building up the paranoia in her brain.

She started looking all around her, to make sure that no one had been listening. She limped to the open window and latched it. Then she secured the door. She would not move out of the room until morning, she thought. Sleep was out of question. As she watched over Tatya, her mind wandered back to the fateful day when Kasturi had been found hanging from the branch of a tree.

CHAPTER EIGHTEEN

The Return of Reality

Sagar opened his eyes waiting for the headache to burst through his temples but it did not come. He was actually feeling better. He rubbed a hand over his face; he hadn't shaved in five days.

Suddenly, he remembered he had been naked. He pulled up the blanket covering him and looked at himself: he was covered with some sort of oversized sweat pants and a pink T-shirt. Situation was worse than he had surmised. Not only had he been buck naked yesterday, but someone had also taken the liberty of dressing him. He sat up and balanced himself on his outstretched hands. He debated with himself about getting up. He reasoned that if he had to relieve his bladder he would have to walk to some sort of toilet. Another disturbing thought caught up. If he had been here for a couple of days, who had helped him with his daily chores? He checked tentatively for the presence of a urine catheter or a diaper. There was neither and the underwear was also missing. He cursed under his breath. He swung his legs off the bed.

A pair of new rubber slippers had been placed there by his considerate benefactor. He put them on and shuffled towards the door, half expecting it to be locked. But it wasn't. He pushed it ajar and walked out to find himself in a big open space. He looked around but there was no one to be seen. The place was eerily quiet and still.

Somewhere nearby Sagar could make out the sound of a latch being opened. He ducked back into his room before anyone could see him. he stood behind the door and peeked out from the slight space he had left open. A man came out of a room just across the veranda, buttoning his shirt. He was followed by a woman wearing nothing from waist down. A thin golden line caught the sunlight and glittered around her flat waist. A clump of black shone between her legs as she turned in the direction of the doctor's room. Sagar clamored back behind the door. He could hear them speaking indistinctly. There seemed to be some altercation going on as the voices had increased in crescendo. He hazarded a look again. The woman, absolutely at ease in standing naked except for a red blouse and the waist band, had her hands over her hips. Her hair, long and wavy was tumbling all around her in chaos as she ran her hands through them with exasperation.

The man came dangerously close to the woman but she did not back up in spite of the fact that she was but half his size. The man, unsure of what needed to be done hastily took out some more money from his pocket, and threw it on her face and left, before she could shout some more. Once he was out of the gate, the woman picked up the money, and subconsciously touched the notes to her eyes, as if asking for forgiveness at the sacrilege, and put it inside her blouse. Then she clumped her hair behind her head with both her hands and rolled it into a tight and tidy bun. She took a petticoat hanging on the drying line and put it on, thereby covering herself. Without even breaking a step, she picked up a broom and started sweeping the veranda.

Sagar had no intension of bringing it to the woman's notice that he had been staring at the play of colors on her body for the last ten minutes. But he had to find a toilet. He tried to guess which one of the several doors led to it. Accepting defeat, he shuffled clumsily out of his room. The woman looked up sharply. Immediately, she dropped her broom and ran to help him. He indicated with his little finger that he wanted to relieve himself. The woman held him by his right arm and supported him to the bathroom.

Once inside, Sagar stood still, making no movement to lower his pants, because the woman was standing close to him and was showing no signs of leaving him alone to afford him some privacy. He started to protest but she cut him short by expressing her decision to remain standing right there. Sagar could care less at the moment; his bladder had taken the reins. He lowered his sweat pants just enough to pop out his penis.

This must have been the longest pee he had taken in his life, he thought. When done, he stooped to fill up a mug with water to flush the toilet. The woman stopped him with a slight touch on his back. It was implied that she would clean up after him. Sagar's head was spinning. Whether it was because of the fact that he hadn't eaten for a very long time, or because he had just seen the most beautiful woman in his life naked, was not clear. Nevertheless, he was glad that she was there to help him as he was already feeling tired and extremely hungry.

Once he had lain down again on his bed, he could feel his racing heart returning back to normal. The woman was arranging the blanket on his legs and she had her left profile turned towards him. She looked quite familiar. He had met her before, and had also known her name. The woman, engrossed in her work quickly came to the left side of the bed, and smoothened out the mattress. Sagar peered at her face closely. A strong whiff of musk floated out to him and he knew immediately who she was.

"Kasturi?"

The hands stopped, as if caught off guard. For the first time, she looked at him in the eye as she straightened up. The doctor realized that he was mistaken; although the resemblance could not be ignored. She was not Kasturi. But Sagar could make out the line of moisture gathering at the bottom of the impossibly large doe eyes. The woman hastily picked up the empty water jug, and started walking towards the door. Just at the threshold, she turned and looked at Sagar.

"Charu, doctor, my name is Charu."

****

The nauseous feeling clung to her all day long. Even cooking had become an impossible feat. Simple flavors of cumin and curry leaves pecked her to the edge of throwing up. Lata had no one to ask help from. She was sure that she was finally having the signs and symptoms of the disease which would eventually kill her. She had noticed many changes in her body. For one, she had missed her periods for two months straight. Her otherwise compliant stomach had suddenly turned foe and had made simple tasks exceedingly difficult for her. She dared not to ask Gaurang Sahib as she was sure that he would either not answer or ridicule her to shame. She decided to sleep on it and wished that whatever it was would go away soon.

By the third month, she had been reduced to a bony cage, unable to eat or drink anything. Gaurang was irritated at her sickness. What could possibly make her sick? He had already passed his judgment that his lazy and good for nothing wife had come up with this new façade in order to glean sympathy from him. But when one fine morning she did not turn up with the tray of tea and breakfast, he got up angrily and decided to give Lata a sound thrashing. He could not find her in the kitchen or in any of the rooms. Where was she? Had she absconded with one of the men? Anger boiled up in him and he started imagining his infidel wife in arms of other men. He raged throughout the house, maddened by anger.

On a second thought, he walked towards the back door, which opened to the wash area. The door was ajar. He kicked it open and was getting ready to beat the hell out of his stupid wife. His eyes fell on a bunch of clothes left in the open, right in the middle of nowhere. He walked towards it will the mind of aiming a sound kick at the clothes and making them fly. As he approached closer, he realized that the bunch of clothes was breathing. A spray of yellowish liquid was staining the cemented floor.

Lata was unconscious and her clothes were seeped in sweat. Gaurang bent down and shook her shoulders. When she did not respond, he called out her name. She lay there on the floor unmoving. Her once fitting clothes had become baggy and were slipping down to reveal an extremely emaciated rib cage. Her shoulder bones jutted out and she looked like a skeleton more than a living person.

Gaurang, not sure of what to do, picked her up awkwardly. She felt like a small child in his arms. He carried her inside the house and placed her on the bed. He ran a hand through his hair. He had to do something or else she might die. He surprised himself by feeling sad at this thought. He knew that the doctor was missing and the replacement had yet to join the office. The next doctor was at least 100 km away. He could only think of the nurse back in the PHC who could help him. He raced out of his house and hopped on his bike. He sped to the old nurse's house as soon as he could.

She was outside, still in her night clothes, watering her rose bushes; and finding the PI at her doorsteps so early in the morning could only mean someone was sick. Gaurang parked his bike and walked towards her, barely managed to tell the nurse awkwardly that he had found his wife unconscious in a pool of her own vomit. The kind woman motioned him to sit while she got dressed. She came out after few minutes with her brown bag of first aid; got on the bike balancing herself by placing a hand on the his shoulder.

Once they had reached PI Gaurang's, the nurse got down gingerly, her bones creaking with arthritis. She waddled inside the house and went to the room indicated by Gaurang. Lata was lying half propped up on two pillows, her deep sunken eyes open. Seeing Gaurang in front of her, she started to get up, but the nausea kicked her again as she dissolved into spasms of dry heaving retching. The nurse was looking at her curiously, and asked Gaurang to step outside the room. After what seemed like a long time, she emerged from the room smiling. She walked up to him and told him that his wife had been pregnant for at least three months. When she did not get the reaction she had expected, she just shrugged her shoulders and asked him to drop her off at her house.

On his way back from the nurse's house, Gaurang's numb brain was trying to formulate the news he had just received. Suddenly he was filled with a surge of shame and guilt. For some reason, the last time he had forced himself on her kept coming back to him. Every time he closed his eyes, he could see his devoted wife moving around the house silently like a shadow, never complaining. While going back in her house, the nurse had warned him about the failing health of his wife, and expressed her fears about whether she would be able to pull through with the pregnancy.

Gaurang sat on his bike, his legs stranded on each side, rubbing a hand over his closed eyes and face. He was finding it difficult to think rationally with the feeling of guilt and unfairness he had shown to his simple and demure wife for years. Now, when he was in danger of losing her forever, he could not even bear to imagine his life without her. The boss, Charu, the dead body recently found… everything seemed inconsequential. The moisture on the palm of his hand were tears.

He walked inside the house and found Lata bent over the stove preparing tea. He walked up to her and stood still, unable to gather courage to talk to her. He coughed a little awkward cough and Lata turned, almost tripping the boiling pot of tea. Gaurang couldn't look up and meet her eyes. She was standing cowered waiting for his lash out. Instead, when her husband put a kind hand on her shoulder, she could not contain herself and dissolved into uncontrollable sobs. She held his hand with her own and cried in them. Gaurang's heart ached for the first time in his life. All he could do from stopping himself from crying aloud was to take his thin trembling wife in his embrace and walk her to her rightful place in his room.

For the rest of the day, he kept on holding his wife soothing out the numerous blue and black marks on her body and face, all inflicted by him. There was nothing he could do to overcome the bitter bile of guilt that was rising in his mouth. He had been selfish, and a monster. How could he ever forgive himself? He looked down at his wife, sleeping with her head on his lap, her hands still holding his right hand. He threw back his head and let the tears roll.

CHAPTER NINETEEN

Obituaries

The women gathered in small groups with their food trays. Uma followed her new fried Nargis, who was at the sorting station. She was amazed that there was food for all those who worked there. She saw a young boy walk away in the direction of the office with two plates heaped up with food, assumingly for the manager and the supervisors. She followed Nargis as she went from one counter to another. It seemed the food never stopped coming.

There was the red unpolished rice with which she was familiar, followed by thick yellow lentil soup. On the next counter someone scooped up two boiled eggs dipped in red gravy and put it on her plate. For a moment Uma thought that it had been a mistake, but a quick look at the others' plates told her otherwise. In the excitement of having to come to the factory, she had not been able to eat anything. The aroma of the meal brought water in her mouth. She could hardly wait to find a place to sit and take mouthful of the hot steaming food.

She mixed her rice with the lentils and curry and had a big morsel. She could not believe that she was actually eating a hot meal. It was so appealing that she finished all of it. When she saw that the others were not even half way through, she lowered her gazed and fiddled with her tray. Some women were going back to the counter for a refill. Uma's eyes widened a little bit more. There for more if you wanted? She was too embarrassed to get up and ask for more. Nargis looked at her and encouraged her to go on, with a nod of her head.

Uma went up to the counter and asked for more rice. Immediately the person behind the counter dropped as much rice as she had previously handed out. Uma noticed that the egg curry counter had been removed. But the lentils were still available. She asked for some and the lady behind the counter poured out two ladles full of steaming lentils on her rice. A very happy Uma came back to her place and this time she partook in the meal with a slower pace. Around 3 pm, the women gathered on the third floor to resume work.

Uma learned to sort the sea shells as Nargis taught her the names of the different types. She held the various daily little shells and followed it with exotic names. Shark eye, baby's ear, lettered olive, whelk, conches, cockles, clams…the list was exhaustive, but Uma was a quick learner. She was amazed that the shells which had always been an inevitable part of her life had more than one million varieties.

There was a general sense of wellbeing amongst the women, laughing and satisfied with their stomachs full. They spoke about drunken husbands and callous children. The mother-in-laws were the vamps by a unanimous vote. Occasionally someone burst into a laugh at a joke. By the end of 5 pm, the women had started to get up and store away their handiworks. The supervisor was counting and labeling the final products. All the final items were stacked in cardboard cartons with bubble wraps to protect them during transportation. Everyone lined up all along the perimeter of the room and Uma followed.

A silence fell in the room as each woman went up to the supervisor and collected the day's worth of labour. Each worker was asked to sign their initials or put their thumb impressions against their names. Uma being literate could write her name, and so she did with pride, as she collected 200 rupees. The notes were crumbled and a little worn from the edges, but it was money. Uma was beyond herself. This seemed too good to be true. In her euphoria, she failed to notice the quick glances the women were throwing at the supervisor. Many lingered back even after they had received their money.

Nargis, who was right behind Uma, nudged her to keep walking without stopping. As she turned to ask what was the reason for such sudden haste, Nargis, her eyes huge with fear, quietly put a finger on her lips; still urging Uma to be quiet. The abrupt change of ambience and nature in the women was surprising. Nevertheless, she tucked the money in her blouse and started climbing down the stairs. Few women stopped at the second floor and walked towards the locked door. Again, Nargis poked Uma with her finger to move on without asking questions.

Once out of the building, Nargis held Uma and half dragged her into the bus, obviously belonging to the factory, with the large logo of a red conch drawn on a sea blue background, painted on its body. Uma was getting a bit paranoid by her behavior. Nargis chose the seat right next to the door and pulled Uma's hand to make her sit next to her. A few other women followed and seated themselves randomly. Uma looked outside and found that many were just standing outside the building with nothing to suggest that they were home bound. She turned to Nargis with the questions ringing in her head. Again, she put a finger on her lips and asked her to keep quiet.

As much as Uma tried, she couldn't remember any frightening incidence. For her, it had been an exceptionally good day. The bus moved on as it snaked the indigo colored sea coast. Uma could see the boats hobbling on the waves, their lights appearing and disappearing like the fire flies hovering on the nearby trees. The salty humid breeze was strangely cool, indicating it could rain tonight. Uma watched as the sun dipped in the rich blue leaving it crimson for a few minutes before the sky turned a rich color of pink, and then gray.

Uma turned to her new friend again, who had been uncharacteristically quiet. She wondered what could possibly be wrong as Nargis had begun to cry softly. Her eyes were tightly shut and her lips were moving in silent prayer. Soon, the bus slowed down near Momin Pada and Nargis got up in haste and almost ran out of the door without a word or greeting. Uma was hurt and perplexed in equal proportions. She watched as Nargis made her way towards her part of town, her small plastic bag held close to her chest, and her head bowed down.

When the bus took off, Uma saw Nargis frantically waving out to her. Uma waved back, momentarily relieved that there was probably nothing amiss and hoping she had practically cooked up the whole re-actions in her head. If she had looked on, she would have seen Nargis running after the bus for quite a distance shouting out to her friend. If only someone could have managed to tell her that she was 'the new girl' and that her life was on the verge of collapse.

****

Charu fanned the pieces of wood urging them to catch the flame. Within a few minutes she had kindred enough wood to help her cook up a meal. She knew that the doctor was hungry. He had managed to finish off all the fruits she had kept on the table. She was a little hurt when he had called her Kasturi; although she knew she mirrored her elder sister. She had assumed that the doctor will remember her… everyone else did! She had been told several times that once someone had seen her, he could not get her out of their heads. The flattery had made her feel good in the beginning. But as time went by and the ardent lovers started to spurn her and get married with 'decent' women, she realized that those empty words were the tool men used to glean sexual gratification from her. Later, she learned how to fake interest and found out that men were far simpler than given credit for.

She belonged to one of the backward classes of the town. And like most of her neighbors, the kitchen went cold for days. Only when her sister would bring home the money she got from the factory, their mother would take pains to light the fire and cook up a simple meal of mashed rice and lentils. On good days there was half an egg for her.

Her sister Kasturi would refuse to eat, saying she had had her fill in the factory. Charu remembered worrying why her sister was growing progressively listless and skinny if it's true that she was having good food at the factory. Then one day, to everyone's surprise and happi-ness, Kasturi came home with five thousand rupees. None of them had ever seen so much money at once. She told her mother and sister, that she had been selected for a drug trial by a very big company. When her mother's smile faltered, she went on to explain that she wasn't the only person picked, that other women below the age of forty were asked to equally volunteer. They were seen by a very 'good woman' who had convinced them that the medicine was a vitamin pill and would only do them good.

The money was the biggest incentive. They were promised a sum of five thousand at the beginning of the trial, and another ten thousand if they continued for three months. If her mother had been reluctant, the mention of the money had probably changed her mind, because she walked up to Kasturi and hugged her. Charu on the other hand was more practical and knew that there were no free lunches. She tried to find out herself what the factory was up to but she was never allowed inside the perimeters. After getting enrolled in the study, Kasturi started looking and feeling better. She attributed the turn in her health to the magic pill they were given at the end of the day. Even the skeptical Charu had to agree that her sister was happier than before.

At the end of the three months, Kasturi came home with the promised ten thousand rupees, and everyone believed that their days of hardship and hunger were finally over. Kasturi continued to go to the factory. If any, her urge to rush back to work was overwhelming. Every day when she came back, her newly gained buoyancy would have vanished. Gradually, she became mute and forlorn. She would answer vaguely when asked and would turn hostile if stopped from going to work.

Things spun out of control the day Kasturi collapsed on her way to the factory. The onlookers confirmed that she had acted strangely with her arms flinging in paroxysms of spasms, as her eyes rolled back into her head. Few empathetic villagers had carried her to the PHC. Charu had been informed of her sister's predicament by a neighbor. She had run all the way to the clinic. The doctor, his sleeves rolled above his elbows was trying to push a strange looking yellow tube in her convulsing sister's mouth. Two other people were holding her down as the nurse pushed a syringe full of some medicine in her vein. The convulsions stopped immediately followed by a deep throaty noise which frightened Charu more than the former.

The doctor had written down some orders on a piece of paper and handed it to the nurse. Then he had turned towards her and asked her a question which did not make any sense to her at all. She had stared back at him, mute, and unable to answer even when he had repeated the question. The doctor had just raised his eyebrows, shrugged his shoulders and moved past her to attend to the line of patients.

After a day, Charu escorted her sister out of the clinic. She had not had any more convulsions, but it seemed that she had lost some part of her soul. Her eyes were glassy and her lips were cracked. Over the next few days she refused to eat or sleep. The once fair and chirpy girl had been reduced to a walking dead body. Neither her mother, nor Charu could find any way of helping her.

Then one day, a smartly dressed woman came to their house. So out of place were her heels and formal clothes that all the children from the neighborhood had gathered around their house, and peeked in from the windows as if watching an exotic animal. The woman explained that she was the manager of the factory and had come to check on Kasturi as she was concerned. She was extremely jovial and seemed to radiate goodwill and charm. She requested to see Kasturi who was lying in one corner, bundled in as many blankets as they could manage. Without any reservations the woman walked up to Kasturi and sat down right there on the dirt floor beside her. Kasturi, sensing someone near her turned her head.

Finding the manager right beside her in her house, Kasturi had hastily pulled back the covers, and thrown herself in the woman's arms. Charu had never seen her sister cry like that. She refused to let go of the woman and kept on apologizing repeatedly for something she had either said or done. The woman kept patting her back and soothing out her hair, murmuring something in undertones. She must have said something really encouraging, because Kasturi immediately stopped crying and looked at the woman with disbelief. When the woman repeated what she had said, Kasturi started laughing and crying at the same time. The woman hugged her one last time and then stood up, brushing off the dirt stuck to her pants. As she started to take leave, Charu walked behind her, intending to know what she had said to make her sister behave like that. But the woman instead of answering had looked at her from head to toe and nodded appreciatively. Before she could formulate the question, the woman had already taken off in her car.

The next day, Kasturi seemed to have been restored to her prior good humour miraculously. She kept repeating that she had been offered an opportunity which was one in a million. But she refused to give any other information. She was busy packing all her merge belongings in a battered suitcase which had belonged to their father. She explained that she had to be away for about a week because of some factory related work. And with just that and no more explanation, she had left the house.

Charu, although the younger one, was not too excited about the whole thing; and she wished to get an opportunity to talk to her sister, but their poverty had refrained them from possessing any mobile phones. Her mother was also getting agitated. At the end of the said week, a postman came to their doors and gave them a letter from Kasturi, in which she had mentioned that she was doing well and that she might be required to stay away for some more days. The postman also handed over five thousand rupees to Charu, saying that it was a money order from her sister. Charu checked the stamp on the letter and realized that it was from Mumbai. The money was successful in soothing out whatever worries were keeping her mother awake.

Soon, weeks turned into months, but there were no more letters or money from Kasturi. One night, Charu was awakened by a sound of someone scrapping the window. Thinking that it was one of the notorious boys from the neighborhood, she had decided to ignore it. She had turned her back to the window and pulled a pillow over her head. The next day, she was awakened by rapid and loud rapping on her door. Her mother was also awakened and both of them had rushed out to find out what was wrong.

At first, they couldn't make out anything of the small crowd that had gathered around their house, as Charu looked from one face to another. They instinctively raised their eyes to look at something high above. Had it not been for the familiar clothes, Charu would never have recognized her sister. She was hanging from the neem tree and oscillating mildly with the wind. The noose had cut off all the blood from neck down, making her head perfused with blue blood and her eyes, red shot with innumerous small hemorrhages. Her lips seemed to be drawn away from her teeth, as if she was smiling. The neck, unnaturally elongated due to hanging had almost snapped into two.

A loud thud resonated beside her and she turned to find her mother lying unconscious on the ground. She rushed to her side and tried to shake her awake. Many of the women gathered around Charu as she burst into incoherent ranting, beating her chest in grief, as they realized that the mother had died, not able to take in the shock of her daughter's death.

Someone had informed the police and a siren was sounding far away, making its way in the narrow lanes of one of the most forgotten parts of the town. Charu did not even look back at her sister, even when they cut the rope and carried her down. When the PHC van had come and carried away her dead family, she had just walked behind it all the way to the clinic. By the time she reached, the doctor had already finished examining the corpses.

Charu did not remember falling unconscious in the arms of the doctor. But she did remember that kind hands had picked her up and carried her to the only bed with a mattress on it. She remembered the warm embrace in which she had dug her head and cried for the loss of all the people she valued most in the world. Over the next few years, Charu had burned with unanswered questions regarding her sister's death. On several occasions she seemed to have scratched too close for comfort and had had suspicious looking people follow her to her house.

She had decided to ask the PI for help. The PI had taken one look at her and expressed his unspoken part of the deal in return for protection. In a way, Charu had been grateful to the philandering policeman for having introduced her to the world of prostitution. It was clear to Charu, that although the higher caste men would not accept water from her hands, they did not have the same reservations when it came to having sex with her. Charu, charismatic and feisty as ever accepted the way of life quickly in order to survive, but she never gave up on her sister. Also, she never forgot the doctor, nor did she forget the question he had asked her the day her sister had been brought to the clinic with convulsions. Now she knew what the doctor had wanted to know.

"Since when was she on?"

CHAPTER TWENTY

Good lives matter

As Charu stirred the pot of rice boiling in the pot, she whipped a tear which had gathered around her eyes. it had nothing to do with the onions she was chopping for the curry. How could she have missed the clear signs of her sister's de-escalating health? After losing her father to the same poison, she should have picked up the signs since the very first day. The unusual out of the place euphoria followed by the convulsions of withdrawal were right there in front of her. In a way, she had failed her sister and her mother. Now, she was alone and there was no fear of losing anything. She had made up her mind to go to the root of the web of drugs which had snared her innocent sister and killed her.

The warm memories of being close to the doctor, many months ago, helped her in pushing back the negative feelings. When she had heard that the doctor was missing and probably dead, just like the previous one, she had been crazed with grief. Then one day, her photographer friend, had called her about a half drowned man who had uttered the name of her sister, before becoming unconscious. She had rushed to the beach on a borrowed scooter. The photographer had dragged the man out of the returning tide. It was fortunate for the doctor that he had been washed up on the uninhabited part of the beach.

Charu, without missing a beat, called the ward boy of the PHC whom she trusted, and asked him to come to the beach with the van.

Between the three of them, they had picked up the doctor and drove him to Charu's new house in a better and cleaner part of the city, although separated from those belonging to the higher caste folks.

In the shroud of night, they had taken off the wet clothes and warmed him with blankets and whatever they could find. The ward boy had left in haste afraid of being caught. The photographer had followed but not before Charu made them swear to secrecy. She also made it clear, that if they breached the deal they would never be able to sleep with her again. The men, already addicted to her, agreed at once and returned to their blemish free worlds, leaving her with the half dead doctor.

She had cared for him with all her heart, taking care of keeping him hidden, especially from her raucous lover, PI Gaurang. The doctor had developed a nasty fever which had raked his body for five days before leaving him quite weak. Gradually, he had started to come back to his normal condition. The spark of intelligence had returned to his deep brown eyes, much to her happiness. Today, for the very first time, she had ignited the kitchen stove to cook a hot meal for her friend. She had reprimanded herself millions of times for giving a thought to a possible future with the doctor. Not only was she a scheduled tribe woman, she was also an outcast. There was no way that the doctor would even look at her.

****

Mahesh had opted to stay back at home. He had told his brothers that he was feeling poorly and he wished to rest. Although everyone in the household knew that Mahesh was feeling anxious about his wife. This was the first time since his marriage that Uma had been away for such a long time. As the evening approached, Mahesh started to pace all around the compound of the house.

Many times he attempted to go and fetch Uma himself. Then he checked and chided himself for being so cynical. As such, there were no ferries after six in the evening.

By each passing moment, Mahesh became exceedingly restless. His parents tried to calm him down, but he shouted at them for being insensitive. Around seven, Mahesh had had it. He was already on his way out when he saw Uma walking towards the house. Unconscious of her surroundings, Uma had let her pallu slide away from her head. Something had made her jubilant. She was skipping and running, her lips curved into a happy song. When she was about a hundred feet from the house, she suddenly looked up and saw Mahesh. If possible, her smile brightened as she doubled her steps and came running towards him.

Mahesh hid his worry and smiled at whatever was making his wife so happy. Uma re-enacted the whole day to him, frame by frame. She skipped the part about Nargis behaving strangely as she was sure that things would be different the next day. Once inside the house, she took out the two hundred rupees and handed it to her mother-in-law. Then again, she narrated the whole experience once again for the benefit of the others. She declined dinner stating that she was still full with the enormous lunch she had had that afternoon.

Once on her bed, Uma curled off to sleep almost instantly. Mahesh came to the room after some time and climbed in bed beside his wife. He tucked her with the blanket which had slipped away from her body. Then he spooned up to her and fell asleep. The night was cool and silent. But Mahesh was struggling to keep horrifying dreams at bay. He dreamt of horrifying demons and watched with horror as they dragged his wife into inferno. He got up with a start at three in the morning, his mouth dry and his lips chapped. He rarely had nightmares, so this was very unsettling for him. He looked at Uma snoring lightly and lost in her own pleasant dreams.

Mahesh was not psychic. If he was, he would have correlated the sudden occurrence of the dreams with the feeling of imminent loss and doom which was rearing its head in his mind.

****

Ratan was certain that the Lord was the one who had introduced

Phooli to the poison. He had left home with his heart ablaze with the fire of revenge. He was very sure of the plan he had worked up in his mind and it had made complete sense to him. But now, sitting in this non-descript filthy room he was completely lost. Multiple times he had emptied the contents of the plastic bag on the bed and stared hard at the bottles as if daring them to answer his questions. The bottles, mute and unanimated bore silent witness to the injustice that had been served to Ratan and his dead wife.

Since time immemorial, the poor had always been expendable. Their life or death mattered less than the dogs the rich had kept as pets. He knew all this, having narrowly escaped a similar result by a hair's breath. Had it not been for Keva Bai, he would still be lolling in the unending darkness of drugs. Ratan collected and counted the bottles yet again and put them back in the bag. Then he laid down, and closed his eyes.

It was Ratan's plan to go to the factory and meet Keva Bai. If any-body could tell him about the bottles, it was her. He had also planned to put before her the possibility of the involvement of the Lord in the shady business. His mind drifted back to his Phooli. His heart ached as his wife's jovial innocent face came in front of his eyes, only to be overshadowed by her sunken lost eyes, her bruised, bleeding, and avulsed finger nails, as she clawed the walls in order to escape. He had failed her.

He let the grief take hold of him completely. So real was the heart-ache that Ratan doubled up. He had been the real culprit, unable to know the signs of his poor wife. His ignorance has good as killed her. But it was time now, that the criminals had to be brought out in the open. Their masks to be removed and their real faces exposed out to the world. The stab wound on his left side throbbed with agonizing pain as he bent, dulling his resolve by small measures. Ratan had decid-ed to let nothing come in his way of his mission.

He stood in front of the cracked and spotted mirror and checked the wound. It had a scab of dried blood on it. He knew that it was what was damping the flow of blood. Ratan took a long fresh dhoti, still stiff with starch. Then he wrapped it tightly around his waist, each turn sending a shooting pain down his groin. When he was done he tore the free end in two horizontally and used the frayed edges to knot and hold the bandage in place. Gradually the pain settled. He checked the efficacy of his work by turning sideways and bending down. The wound did not sting. For all that mattered, Ratan was ready to fight for justice for his Phooli or die trying.

CHAPTER TWENTY-ONE

The Bapats

A good number of years back his childhood friends Keshav and Bhima had come back to town for their long awaited vacation. Unlike Ratan, these boys had had the luxury of being born rich, but friendship together had never been affected by such. Unlike their father and orthodox uncle, the boys were like any other their age. The twins, inseparable since birth had managed to secure seats in foreign university in London. In their absence, Ratan had become forlorn and depressed. With neither parents alive, and with the merge income by fishing, he had almost given up completely on life.

Then, one day, while he was gearing up to go fishing in the deep sea, he saw the other young men rubbing salt on their mouth-gums. Considering that the substance was plain simple salt, the secrecy surrounding it was very surprising to Ratan. He had asked one of the men about it and he had denied the whole issue with an expressionless face. Once deep in the sea, two men overpowered him and took him with surprise. After sustaining a few well-placed punches and slaps, he had been threatened by the men that if he ever mentioned the event of the salt to anyone on dry land, they would make sure he joined his dead parents sooner than he could say 'God'.

Ratan had remained quiet. He was smart enough to know when silence was the only tool of survival. But he had made up his mind about testing the substance himself. One of the fishermen had been sleeping at a corner on the deck with an almost empty plastic wrapper lying near him. Ratan had slipped it unnoticed in his pocket. During the next few hours on the boat, he saw the fishermen boasting and laughing with augmented courage and euphoria. When the sea became rough and the waves got bigger and more threatening, the men just laughed and steered the boat right into the massive waves. The catch was good and Ratan thought that the happiness had something to do with that.

When they roped the boat in the dock, the euphoria had reduced by several degrees. The men looked fidgety and agitated. All the good humor had vanished leaving them miserable and confused. They were less concerned about their catch which had already started to whither and get limp, than making their way to the Lord's house. Ratan for the world of it, couldn't make out either head or tail of the whole issue. When he saw that most of men had forgotten all about the shrimps, crabs and lobsters, he gathered them all and decided to sell it to the restaurants. Expecting a retribute at any moment, Ratan had spent the whole afternoon in the market looking over his shoulder. But no one came in his direction. Everybody seemed to have forgotten about the morning. The slight ache on his abdomen and the cut on his lips reminded him that it was true enough.

Later in the evening, when he had reached his mud hut, he had taken out the partially full packet from his pocket. He tried to smell it, but there was no smell to associate the curious substance with anything that he knew of. Cautiously he took a pinch of the white powder and put it on his tongue. As soon as the powder met his tongue, numbness spread on it. He decided to try it just as he had seen the men do in the sea. He took a chunk of it and rubbed it on his gums and waited. Nothing spectacular was happening. In fact, his mouth was filled up with a bitter taste which was unpalatable. He rolled the rest of the powder and shoved it under his pillow. After a couple of minutes he realized he felt very happy. Whatever had happened, he was richer today, having been lucky to get all the catch for himself. Life was wonderful! He was alone and king of his own kingdom. He was unbeatable. He was young and healthy…soon he would buy the same damn boat which he had ferried today. He was going to punch the man on his face… and… and… Ratan wanted to run out and shout. He thought that was a great idea, until he managed to fall over a chair he hadn't noticed was there before he could carry out any of his ambitious plans.

By the next morning, it was clear to young Ratan that the powder, whatever it was, was magical. It made him feel like a man. He could conquer the world with it. Maybe it was some secret medicine the others were using for vitality and stamina? Ratan decided to use his stash cautiously, because he did not want to enrage the other burly fishermen by asking them for more.

He had no need to worry, because the source walked up to him. It was a day like any other when Ratan was anchoring his small dingy, that he was approached by the most beautiful woman he had ever laid his eyes on. Her silky black and straight hair was blowing gracefully in the breeze. She had worn clothes which Ratan had only seen actresses wear in the talkies. He thought she was mistaken when she came up to him and called him by his first name. Ratan, tongue-tied had just nodded. She had asked him to follow her and he did so without question. When they were near a car, a man ran out to open the door for the woman as she slid inside gracefully, the slit in her skirt riding higher exposing expensive lace stockings. Ratan couldn't help but look at the striking play of colors on the woman's body. He was standing outside, unsure of what was expected of him next. The woman put her head out of the car window and asked him to get in the car. Ratan followed the order.

The car was big and black with matching leather covers in the interiors. He kept his eyes averted and the woman laughed at his discomfiture. Suddenly she placed her white manicured hand on his thigh forcing him to look up at her. His mind was racing with all possibilities. He was nervous as he had not had much experience with women ever in his life… what was he supposed to do? Should he keep his hand on top of hers? Was he supposed to close his eyes and kiss her the way he had seen in the movies? He was shaking with a mixture of excitement and nervousness. He was sure that the woman had come to seduce him. Why him? The question did not matter to him at all at this time, he thought.

By the time Ratan had played all the scenes in his head, the woman had removed a folder from her bag. In the local dialect, she started explaining to Ratan about some pharmaceutical drug experiment they were conducting. She added that the company was ready to pay five thousand rupees at once, if he accepted and later twenty thousand more, if he continued to be a part of the study. Without his asking, the woman told him in hushed tones, so that the driver could not overhear, that it was the same medicine he had been taking to make himself feel better. It was indeed a wonderful medicine and a type of harmless vitamin.

Ratan was relieved and happy beyond measure. He was going to get a lot of money for taking a medicine which only made him feel good. He agreed and without concerning himself about reading the document handed out to him, he signed wherever the woman asked him to. She fished out two complete packets of the medicine and passed it to him, asking him to be extremely discreet, as the company was choosing only healthy and able bodied people. If the news about the cash money leaked out, he might lose the opportunity of getting the promised twenty thousand rupees.

Saying so, the woman opened her bag and counted out ten notes of crisp five hundreds and handed them to Ratan. The money felt alien in his hands. After his father's death, he had never seen a five hundred rupees note ever in his life. Now, he not only had them, he had ten of them.

On his way home, he had repeatedly felt for the packets in one pocket and the money in the other. It was all true, he kept telling himself. What could be better that this? In a few weeks' time his friends Keshav and Bhima were coming back. Maybe he would share this fantastic piece of luck with them, although they did not need it. Everything in their lives was good.

When Ratan did not come to meet them at their arrival, the brothers were surprised. When they had spoken about three weeks back, telling him about their vacation, he had been thrilled and over the moon. He had promised to collect them from the railway station. When they aligned from the train, there was no Ratan to greet them. Supposing that he had been taken in by work, they had let the matter rest. But when their friend did not pick up their calls and was absent even on the fourth day, they were worried. It was so very out of character for Ratan to ignore them like that.

Unknown to their parents and uncle, they had slipped out of their house in search of their friend. He was neither at the docks, nor was he at the market. His usual place was empty. They made way to his house. It was dark inside and no one answered to their calls or knocks. They were just about to return, when they heard a faint sound coming from the hut. The door was open but they could barely make out the figure of a thin man lying on the floor. From the smell of the place, it was evident that he had neither bathed, nor had he left the hut to relieve himself in days. The brothers tipped around dried feces and snaking rivers of urine and reached the man.

A closer look confirmed that he was indeed Ratan. He was mumbling something and was incoherent. The brothers could not understand as to what had happened to their friend to cause this level of deterioration. Nevertheless, they hauled him from the ground, and carried him to their car. Rattan kept fighting them like a cornered animal, before finally succumbing to seizures.

The boys, studying medicine, finally realized what was wrong with him. They shone light in his eyes. His pupils were wide and non-reacting. His gums were red and hemorrhagic. There was evidence of dried up blood on his nose, suggesting that he had had a recent episode of epistaxis. The brothers knew that their friend was showing signs of cocaine overdose followed by an extreme reaction to sudden withdrawal.

They had been unfortunate enough to have grown in a place where every other youth was a victim. No one knew how they got their stash. What everyone knew was, that the Bapat family was the only one who were standing against this rising antisocial crime like a wall of solid stones. For years, the family had run several NGOs and camps for educating the youths on the dangers of the drug. The police had been donning various caps as per their convenience. Sometimes they would become law abiding, and sometimes against it. But what was always constant was the bitterness the Bapat family had to the abuse of drugs.

The boys, unsure of the level of care and expertise in their small PHC, had decided to take Ratan to their house, where they had decided to keep him hidden to avoid their father or uncle getting a whiff of it. For the next painful 7 days, the boys tied and gagged their friend as he went wild and convulsed alternatively. A raging fever, an aftermath of withdrawal, left him dehydrated and nearer to death that he ever had been. The friends inserted a tube in his nose and fed him milk and medicines. After the seventh day, Ratan had neither fought against his bonds, nor had he convulsed. The fever had lulled to a mild one. The look of recognition returned in his eyes. It was then, that the Bapat brothers released Ratan and hugged him tightly.

Slowly he had started telling them about the experiment in which he had participated for want of money. But the company had gone bust and had to stop the experiment mid-way. So did his weekly supply of the miraculous vitamin powder. Ratan regaled about the benefits of the medicine and a sort of look of greed flickered in his eyes. Keshav made Ratan understand that what he was taking wasn't a medicine at all. It was a very potent drug and he was addicted to it. He had been a part of a bigger scam in all probability. What benefit could one gain by making a simple fisherman addicted to the drug? None of them had any answer. But they were happy that their friend was back from the jaws of certain death.

Once they were sure that Ratan was clean, they had packed him in their car and drove back to his house. On the way, they crossed a black car and Ratan straightened. The glass was tinted with black film, so he couldn't make out the features of the person sitting inside. He pointed the car out to them excitedly and said it was the same one in which the mysterious beautiful woman had come to meet him. The boys had said nothing, but exchanged knowing glances. Once back in their house, Keshav and Bhima were in turmoil. They knew exactly who the person was in the car. They decided to take their mother in loop. She was the only one who was marginally tolerant to the so called backward class people.

The next day they walked into her office. Keva Bai was pleasantly surprised to see her boys in the factory, as she fondly called the building. As Keshav locked the door behind them, Keva knew that this was not a casual meeting. The boys rearranged the chairs to sit closer to their mother. When they were sure that no one was overhearing, they started telling her about Ratan and the woman who was in the middle of all of it. The color in Keva's face started to become redder by the minute. Her nares flared in apparent anger, and her eyes lost all the softness. That moment, she was neither a mother nor a wife. She was simply someone who was angry that her sons had to deal with something like that. She could not believe her ears when they told her the name of the person who had been circulating drugs amongst the youth in the name of some pharmaceutical scam.

Keva stood up and strolled towards the window. She pulled down the vines and glanced outside. Sure, the black car was parked right outside the building. There was nothing else to be done, determined Keva. She asked the boys to stay, while she picked up the telephone and placed a call. In no time, a woman came to the room. Although the brothers had not seen the woman who had actually played the role of the peddler, her clothes and innocent beauty made them guess she must be. She was smiling brightly when she came in, but one look at Keva, wiped away the smile, and replaced it with a fear so palpable that the boys started to feel uncomfortable as well.

Keva addressed her as Mohini and asked if it was her car in the parking. Mohini will her head bowed low just nodded. Keva Bai sprung up from her chair and crossed the table in two strides. In no time she was in front of the woman who took a step back, her hands extended out in front of her face ready to wave off any blow. Keva Bai held the woman's wrists with one hand and pulled them away from her face, and with her right hand she slapped the woman hard. She repeatedly slapped her till the woman was reduced to tears, her elegantly lined eyes smudging to unsightly globes, her set straightened hair in disarray, and her left cheek red with the assaults.

Keshav and Bhima, well accustomed to their otherwise docile mother's anger held her back, allowing the terrified Mohini to run for her life. Once she had made a hasty retreat, the brothers gently cajoled their mother to her chair. A throbbing vein in her neck indicated a surge of blood pressure. Keshav, anxious for his mother's health, pleaded with her to be calm, while Bhima fetched a glass of cold water for her. After a while, when she had calmed down, tears started flowing from her eyes. Both brothers knew where this grief was coming from. Keva had lost her younger brother, not long back to this same poison. Since then it had been a sort of her mission to do her best to curb the curse which was present everywhere in the state. Later, the boys came to know that Mohini had been working right under their noses for a while now. Keva Bai expressed her heartfelt gratitude to her boys for pointing out the wolf amidst the sheep.

Keva Bai had requested a meeting with her boys' friend Ratan, in order to apologize personally. The meeting was arranged and Ratan had been overwhelmed by the kindness Keva Bai had showered on him; and learning that she had humiliated and fired the woman who was behind all the mischief, made him feel grateful. For the next week, the trio of the friends was inseparable. Ratan was happy to see that even their father and uncle were seemingly more tolerant to his presence. Again, everything had sorted themselves out for him and he was happy again.

Soon, it was time for the boys to leave. Somehow around that time, Ratan began to sense a subtle change in his friends. They were less cheerful and spoke little. Ratan had put it down to their imminent departure. More than once he had walked up on them while they were talking about something in hushed tones, but as soon as they saw him, they would stop talking. The generally silent household had started erupting into unprovoked shouts and fightings. Although the boys never told Ratan anything, it was very clear to him that there was some undercurrent of animosity amongst the family members.

Just a day before their scheduled departure, the boys had informed Ratan that they were going to the city for some urgent business, and declined when he asked permission to join them. Ratan, a little hurt at being kept out of an outing, concluded that this was as far as the Bapats would allow him to get near them. Sharing a claustrophobic car with him was out of question. He had stood at a little distance hidden amidst the bushes when the men came out of the house and got into the car. The boys seemed to be debating with themselves whether to get in the car or not. There was another man with them, whom he had seen several times before, but knew only as a newspaper man.

The five of them were busily arguing on something. Although Ratan couldn't make out the correct words, he could understand that the boys were trying to hold them back, pleading and threatening them in turns. Someone must have called out to them, because the brothers turned towards the person and listened to what was being said. Someone was asking them not to go… pleading, cajoling.

Finally, after dilly dallying for a few minutes, the brothers got in the car. Ratan could see the look of determination mingled with incalculable grief in their eyes. Something about the retreating vehicle felt like a premonition. Ratan felt that he was never going to see his dear friends ever again. Spontaneous tears rolled down his eyes and blurred his vision.

That sense of finality… the foreboding feeling had all been true; all the five had been found dead in the car which had skid off the bridge and dropped fifty feet down into a ditch. The water had seeped into the vehicle and fried all the electronic equipment they had been carrying. There was no mention of any possibility of foul play. The postmortem and cremation were finished in a jiffy. It seemed as if Keva Bai, crazed by the loss of her family, had decided to finish everything with the hope of finding some peace and solitude.

After the incident, the atmosphere was replete with rumors of all kinds. Some said that it was the work of some Mafia don. Others pointed out to Mohini, the infamous manageress in the factory. Some brave souls also theorized that Keva Bai may be behind all this, but the latter soon dwindled off. No one could act bereavement… at least not a mother who had lost both her brilliant and kind children. Indeed, it had taken her months to get back on her feet as she took charge of all the family business.

CHAPTER TWENTY-TWO

Seeping out Truth

The boiled raw Papayas, mashed and mixed with freshly ground mustard seeds and red chilies, complemented the thick red and hot grains of rice. On one side of the plate, Charu had placed a generous helping of jackfruit cooked in coconut milk. Sagar not able to resist the tantalizing aroma and taste, downed two helpings, and was hoping for more. Charu was only too happy to serve him. Her heart sang out when the doctor finished his meal, licking his fingers, one at a time. When he started to get up and picked his plate, she stopped him by a slight touch on his wrist, asking him not to bother.

Sagar, drowsy and content after a hearty meal, complied, and turned back to go to his room, but not before throwing a glance in the direction of the container in which Charu had cooked the rice. It was empty. And so were the rest of the utensils. He felt guilty of having eaten even her portion of food. He made a mental note to inform her that he had decided to leave as he was well enough to walk. He did not want to be a burden to her any further. He also realized that she had sheltered him with significant risk to her own life. He did not want to risk any more lives.

Already he was filled with guilt to have Revathi compromised by giving her the actual PM reports and the photographs. At that moment, when he had seen the woman, in her big black car moving to and fro, undoubtedly in search of him, he was sure that his suspicions were not baseless. He had been following the woman and her activities ever since Kasturi had been found hanging from the tree.

The pattern had been as clear as day light. Poorest of the poor youths in fairly good health and in huge need of money were carefully selected by the gang. Sagar believed that the people, previously involved in the scam were given some incentive in return of pointing out the most eligible people. The people, all hard workers and sole breadwinners of the family were introduced to cocaine under the alias of a beneficial and entirely harmless medicine. The modus operandi repeated from here on.

The 'free' samples handed out to them with specific instruction as to how to use, were supplied to the unaware victims for almost two months, by which time the ignorant people were already addicted. The next step was to cook a story about the 'company' going turtle and stopping the free access to the drug. Also the money stopped because it was promised to them if the study was finished. Driven mad by withdrawal and quickly dwindling reserves of money, these youths were ready to go to any lengths and depths to get a single dose of the drug. It is then when these hapless men and women were forced to become carriers or as locally known, the mules, to smuggle moderate quantities of drugs across borders.

The drug was often carefully packet in small pill sized bottles which could be swallowed or concealed in other body cavities. The resilient ones were kept in captivity, nurtured and fed like cattle. The weaker ones or the rebels were killed and dropped in the sea. All these theories were mere assumptions, Sagar knew. He had a fairly good idea as to who was the person pulling the strings. But he had no way of proving anything.

It was rumored that the journalist who was killed along with the other members of the Bapat family, had strong incriminating evidence against the kingpin. But the said photographs were never found. The camera, washed useless was found without the film reel. The case, like numerous others, including the suspicious mutilated washed up bodies, had in all probability been buried and forgotten. Sagar had deliberately left the picture of the particular article for Revathi to find. He hoped that the smart journalist would be able to connect the dots. But, for the meantime, he needed to go to the safe house. He mulled over the safest way to go there, but his eyes were getting heavier. Within a few minutes he was asleep. Pressing issues like running away from certain death could wait.

****

Tatya was eating an exquisitely sweet mango. Every now and then he would check if anyone was making his or her way towards the ward. He had all the intensions to finish the mango before the strict nurse would come and scold him just as if he was a naughty school boy; doing everything except using the cane on him. He sucked the seed swallowing the last drop of the nectar. He quickened his actions as he noticed the bobbing blue and white cap of the nurse. He threw the seed out of the window and wiped his hands on the hanging bed-sheet, just as she entered the ward, limping on her bad leg. There was a new person with her today. The cheerful woman felt like a cold shower on hot days. Her smile and cheerful disposition contrasted with the grump of the nurse. By the look of it, she seemed to be the new medical officer, appointed in place of the absconding or missing doctor. Tatya would have preferred a young, beautiful woman over anyone, on any day.

He had been admitted a few days back in a condition of coma with an infected finger and high fever. He was told how two of his colleagues and the nurse had carried him between them. He also knew that the nurse had taken care of him diligently, often staying back at nights. Her selfless acts had forced him to see the old nurse in a new light.

The lady doctor greeted Tatya with a dazzling smile and checked his vitals and progress reports. It seemed to her that the constable was well enough to leave the hospital. The nurse was looking at him with hands on her hips. He had forgotten to wipe the pulp from his mouth, which he did sheepishly. The nurse pointed out to the new doctor that his sugars were still uncontrolled. She seemed to be over eager to please, because she waved off the whole thing as ridiculous, and ordered to discharge the grateful constable. The nurse shrugged and shook her head as it seemed to her that, as one young doctor replace another, the young doctors only got worse and more incompetent.

****

Nargis was getting paranoid. Had anyone caught her waving to Uma, the new girl? She had decided not to act as the messiah anymore. But something in the innocence of this young girl had made her motherly heart ready to take the risk one more time. She was not the only one who knew what was going to happen to her. The other women, who had outlived their use and had been serving since the good part of twenty years had been kept under tight security. The hostel meant to be a safe house for them was actually a virtual prison.

Five years back when the bodies started turning up on shores and fishing boats, the mastermind had decided to let things be as they were. The temporarily raised stink had bought them a few precious years of life. Nargis on the other hand was still not adequately 'initiated' to the miracle drug. On several occasions when they had tried to force higher doses down her throat or through her vein, she had run to the PHC in spite of being under the influence.

Thereby, on more than one occasion she had proved that she was a dangerous liability and they needed to keep her closer to themselves. She was the only raw nerve in the thick skinned organization which had not the least of concerns for anyone other than themselves. She had the rare privilege of going back to her home with her three kids and a handicapped husband. They had agreed to her request to go home only if she promised to come back every day and bring new eligible mules.

She was herself guilty of pointing out several girls one of which had been Kasturi. She did it not for the money, but she knew that if she did not, they would not even wait a minute before killing all her family members. Uma had been recommended by someone very close to her own family. She knew the person and was astonished as to how someone could push someone they knew into this hell.

That day, whenever she had laid her eyes on Uma, she was reminded of Kasturi. Kasturi had followed Nargis to the establishment. When she was new, she too had been bedazzled by the huge building decorated with wooden floors and white walls. Nargis knew that they would be served something special that day, as was the routine whenever a new girl joined the pen.

The poor women, who had never had the fortune of having a single meal for days, were seduced easily into a faux comfort zone with good hot food and promise of money. There were many ways the kingpin, or 'the boss' as this person was known, used to trap the mules. Where money or food failed as the bait, sex was used. And in extreme cases when that too failed, the foolproof age old tactics of devotion was used. The boss was a pro in all the games.

There were throngs of people reporting to the boss. Each knew a small part or just one facet of the elusive person, whereas there were several. Even Nargis, having worked in various facilities, playing her part un-obstructively, had never seen the boss. She was not sure that if confronted, she would even recognize the person. The thought that the boss was someone possibly amongst them, or someone she knew and trusted, was a frightening one. After the last body of the pregnant woman had been fished out, Nargis knew that her own days were counted. If they could take out somebody who was so high up in the hierarchy, then she was just a small insignificant pawn.

That night Nargis could not sleep. Her eldest daughter was eighteen, almost the same age as that of Uma. Next month she was going to get married, and on Nargi's insistence she was to shift to a different state with her husband never to turn and look back. She looked at her sleeping daughters and her amputee husband in their bedroom. She had done everything she could to bring food to the house; but at what cost? Indirectly, she was responsible for the death of Kasturi. She could debate with her rational mind all she wanted to, but the stark truth was that she had blood on her hands. How would she show her face to Allah?

She looked again at her children sleeping peacefully, rice and curry resting peacefully in their stomachs, oblivious of the place from where it had come, or at what price. Nargis hid her face in her dress and cried silently. She made up her mind; she was not going to let another innocent woman become the victim of this manslaughter. Her mind had been formulating plans of escape, but now she added details to bring down the factory. She knew that she would probably not live to see her grandchildren once she had done what she was planning to, but that was the only way to ask forgiveness from God Almighty. Her plan was shaky, but the only way out. She had to wait for one more month. She wanted her daughters to be as far from this muck as they possibly could. But for now, she had to talk to Uma.

CHAPTER TWENTY-THREE

Reminiscences

Revathi was trying to read in between the lines. The article was dated correctly. She knew that it wasn't a hoax. Although she had been all of ten years, she remembered the day as clear as yesterday. The damaged camera had been returned to her mother on her request. It was still on the mantle with the photograph of her father hanging on the wall. Out of curiosity she had played 'journalist' with her father's camera; and kept it around her most part of her journalism career to date.

She remembered her father was very particular about carrying extra negatives in case an extraordinary opportunity decided to present itself at unusual places. The article mentioned that no photographs were found in the car, also the camera had been found sans its reel. It was highly improbable that her father would carry an empty camera on such an important mission. That could mean only two things. Either the reel had been taken away from someone who had been investigating the scene, or… Revathi closed her eyes and let her mind be filled in by the persona of her father.

She could see the younger brother of Laxman Rao Bapat, Suketu driving the car, twirling the steering wheel wildly. She could see Laxman Rao's mouth opened in a silent scream. The young boys sitting in the back had yet not realized the gravity of the situation. She waited for the fear to creep in her mind. But surprisingly it was calm and composed. She could see the piercing black eyes of her father thinking fast. The car had climbed the steep bridge. Maybe they were trying to reduce the velocity of the car. They had reached the middle of the bridge when it swung on its front wheels and plunged in the ditch.

She picked up the camera and re-inspected it; just for the energy of fighting for her father's life; then she saw something she hadn't really observed before. Just by the empty film box was another casing looking detachable. She hadn't thought of breaking down the camera before just for the pride of keeping her father's life going through the lens of the piece.

She put her fingers to work on the box and pressed all the seams and sides. Her heart beat fastened as she saw something small and cylindrical through a slight opening. She tore at the seams to get to it. She shone her torch on the black smooth and tightly sealed container. It was a Kodak film; intact, good, and ready to be developed. Obviously, her father had bought a true journalist's camera with a deceptive film cage and the real film container much more obscure.

****

The new girl was just perfect: healthy, eager to please and very poor. It had always amused her when she realized exactly how easy it was to lure such young people with little money and one square meal. Since the headquarters had been shifted to this village, she had recruited more than fifty people out of which several couldn't tolerate the drug, and became dangerously sick. Many had to be cut loose because they were sick from the very beginning; and there were a very small portion of them, who couldn't be bought. They were the ones who were dangerous. But the most damaging ones were those with sudden moral enlightenment. People like Nargis. Both she and Nargis were standing with knives aimed at each other's backs ready to strike if needed. But she decided to brush off the minor issues of rebels and concentrate on her fresh catch.

She had seen and met the husband. Like the rest of the fishermen, he was just as gullible, and more than ok with the idea of his wife earning some extra mullah. Also, she was newlywed; barely over three months. The emotional connection would be non-existential. That would stop the husband from prying when eventually she went missing. She had learnt from experience that engaging women like Phooli was not to be taken lightly. Everyone in the pyramid knew about the potential threat they faced from Ratan, the bereaved husband. The Lord had been very clumsy. First there was the issue of the pregnant woman and then there was Phooli. Grudgingly she had to accept her own failures as well. Kasturi was a loose thread. Even in her death, she had managed to open a can of worms.

Although technically, it had been the foolish and overly cocky and dramatic henchman who had thought that staging a hanging just in front of the victim's house was a bold and loud statement. That is what she had been trying to tell the buffoons, that their actions were not supposed to make either sound or scene. But the gorilla of the man with the brain of a tadpole had only smirked, and did as he wished. In a way, she was pleased that he was dead. The boss could do with lesser of those kinds of people. What the boss needed were people like her.

Mohini, in her new getup, had gone through a nerve racking acid test. She was sure that she would not be recognized in a place where she had never been to. But it was, as the proverb went, a small world. Her short pixie haircut and thick rimmed glasses paired with plaid boring clothes and the white apron would have fooled her own mother, although she did not have one. When she easily created fake documents and gained entry into the small PHC, she had never dreamt of finding someone who knew her there. When the nurse had led her to the depleted hall which was being used as a pathetic excuse for a ward, she had been momentarily shaken by finding herself in front of the constable. She had dared to look directly in his eyes, ready to strike, and if needed finish both the constable and the nurse, in case he showed any signs of recognition. The thin razor sharp cutter in her pocket cut through her skin as she held it tightly in her apron pocket.

The dim witted Tatya couldn't see anything further than his belly and Mohini was relieved when not even a flicker of recognition crossed his face. But there was something in what the nurse had said or asked which had made her alert. She made up her mind to be wary of the nurse for the short period she had planned to be here. She had been placed in this place by the boss to help her stay visibly invisible, and also to field some more dead bodies, expected to float their way to the PHC, because the consignment of mules was supposed to be crossing the seas in a day or two.

Considering the tide and its flow, the boss had estimated that some of the dumped out-of-use or dying mules might make their way to the beach. She had been placed to cover them up. Meanwhile, Mohini had also decided that this was an excellent opportunity for her to prove herself to the boss. She had laid a trap for the absconding doctor and had decided to be prepared with her cutter, to welcome him whenever he was foolish enough to return. The whole fiasco with Kasturi and Ratan had left her favorite pupil status marred. The boss had heisted for the first time, before handing her the next important assignment. The dorky PI Gaurang had been the boss's first choice. Just because he failed to turn up and couldn't be reached the job was passed on reluctantly to Mohini.

She had liked the job at the factory. It was easier for her to get the seasoned women and few old mules, who had escaped the gallows, to become recruiters. It was also easier for her to create a one to one communication with the younger ones. The men just loved her style, and swooned at every word she said. During her brief period in the factory, she had successfully picked up excellent mules; until Ratan turned up with those pesky kids and figured out exactly how she worked. The old hussy had slapped her in front of the boys, and the embarrassment was branded in her mind. She had tried convincing the boss to let her take out Keva Bai along with the rest of the family, but she had just been answered with silence. The boss's silence was more lethal than any act of violence. Silence from the boss meant that the person talking had crossed a line, which they should never have. So, when Mohini got her answer, she decided to never mention this again. No one knew the boss; communication is often by way of text messaging.

It had been almost a month since Uma had been recruited. After the first few hiccoughs, she had settled down to the rhythm of the factory. She had started to look forward to the free food and the daily wages of two hundred rupees. It was time to withdraw the carrots and whip the donkey. She had already placed people in the factory. The pesky giggling girl recruited as the manager and the grumpy supervisor were immature and in adept for anything as delicate as the job of priming the mules. She had not even considered them, even once. In fact, they were absolutely oblivious to the real game which was being played right under their nose. Same could be said about Keva Bai. Mohini smirked as she thought about the day when Keva Bai will be accused and arrested for the crimes she didn't even know about. She was waiting for that day… and it felt tantalizingly near.

CHAPTER TWENTY-FOUR

Comrades

Dr. Sagar went to the bathroom where two buckets of water were already waiting for him. One was half filled with hot water, and the other with cold. He knew that there was no cold water supply facility in more than 80% of the village. Most of the folks had to rely on wells or hand pumps to get water for use. Therefore, the filled up buckets, ready for his use, made him thankful. Charu had hardly spoken to him after the day he had mistaken her for her sister Kasturi. How was he to blame? After the discovery of the poor girl's body hanging just outside her house, there was nothing same ever again. These seemingly unrelated sporadic discoveries of females were superficially discordant.

When Sagar had been asked to rush through her postmortem as well, he was sure that there was more to it than met the eyes. Also, he had attended to the dead girl not so long ago, when she had been brought with unmistakable signs of acute withdrawal. Charu, barely a woman herself was inconspicuous with her simple frock and pigtails. It was very well known, that Charu had taken the easier but looked down upon, way of livelihood. He had not laid his eyes on her since Kasturi's postmortem. That she had taken such a high risk in order to save him came as a surprise to him.

Of all the people, Charu was the least expected to reach out to him in time of need. Sagar realized that some of the bias had come from the fact that the PI Gaurang had been a regular client. But the two weeks in which she had taken care of him with unfaltering devotion, had changed his perspective to a whole new dimension. It was as if Charu had two faces: the one which would become sultry and seductive to enchant men, and another, deeper and more dominant, of a pious God-fearing woman who was intelligent and extraordinarily courageous.

But it was time for him to move on. Staying any longer in her house was invariably going to raise questions, and he might be actually putting her in harm's path.

He finished his bath and dressed in the crisp starched cotton trousers and shirt Charu had got him. He set about to find her. She was neither in kitchen, nor in her own room. He decided to check outside, but Charu had warned him against it. Still, the eerie silence of the otherwise boisterous household was worrying him. Even the hen and ducks were missing. He decided to call out her name, but stopped. What if she was not alone? What if she was right at that moment being forced to keep quiet with the threat of a knife on her throat?

Sagar picked up the washing board as a surrogate of a weapon for self-defense. He could see that the front door was ajar. He crept on the edges, poorly covered by the clothes hanging out to dry on the line. As he inched closer to the door, he could hear a high pitched sound from somewhere far off. It sounded like a woman commanding little children to scoot over. He strained his ears for any other sinister sound. There was none. Nevertheless, with his improvised weapon he dashed out of the door, ready to bang the brains out of anyone who would be stupid enough to come near him.

When he got out into the compound, the scene in front of him rendered his paranoia useless. Charu, with two of her hens hanging upside down from her hands was standing at a distance, her legs apart and her skirt tucked up on her waist, was obviously trying to shout the poultry into submission. The hens had other things on their minds. They escaped as soon as they were put in the coop. Charu turned towards the doctor with the washing board in hand, and broke out in pleas of laughter. Sagar put the board aside sheepishly, and turned to go back in the house. He was glad that he had the sun blasting on his face. He could very well blame the sun for the rising color of his cheeks.

After some time, Charu made her way to the house with three eggs nested in a temporary pouch made of her saree. She quietly crossed the veranda where Sagar was sitting with his hands resting on his lap. Soon, a rich aroma of coconut milk and roasted peanuts filled the house. Charu came out of the kitchen every now and then to gather herbs from her small garden.

Sagar estimated from the position of the sun and the lingering coolness in the air that it had to be around ten in the morning. If he was to reach the safe house, he would have to leave early. He knew that Charu might not take his decision well; but he had to leave, whatever he had to risk. He could not let his decisions harm Charu in any way. Determined, he walked to the kitchen. She was stirring a pot full of red rich gravy in which the three eggs were swimming leisurely. He gave a little discreet cough. Charu, who had been squatting in front of the stove with her saree ridding high up her knees, turned towards him and hastily adjusted her attire.

When she did not offer any opening line, Sagar blurted out his decision to leave right then. To his surprise Charu arched her brows in contemplation and nodded vigorously as if agreeing. Quickly, she dished out two plates with heaps of rice and poured ladles of the still boiling curry on top of each. Two of the three eggs found their way to the plate obviously meant for Sagar. The doctor was not sure where this was going. Finally Charu asked him to sit down and have the food before leaving. Her nonchalance made him feel a little deflated. He sat down as instructed and started mixing the steaming rice and curry together, his fingers getting red with the emitting heat. He had not yet started, when Charu, her plate cleaned out of the last morsel, stood up and left Sagar to finish his meal in peace.

Sagar had placed the plate just beside that of Charu's and washed his hands with the pail of water kept in an old Favicon container. He came out of the kitchen making the plans for his next move. Charu was sitting on the bed on the veranda, her hair tied in a bun and her feet clad in sports shoes. Two bundles were placed at her feet which she was tapping impatiently. The doctor went up to her and motioned at the two bundles. Charu got up and place a pair of men's boots in a fairly good condition near his feet, urging him to put them on.

Without a word of explanation, she went to the kitchen, and came out after some time with several other smaller bundles. On her way out, she locked the door and touched the picture of Jesus Crist handing just outside the kitchen. It was evident that Charu was geared up to leave with him. Sagar wouldn't hear of it and tried to dissuade her. Charu seemed to have turned selectively deaf, and picking up the two bags, she started walking towards the door. A motor car of some sort stopped in front of the house and Charu climbed in and made herself resolutely comfortable.

Sagar had no other way than follow suit. On his way out, he took the bunch of keys hanging near the door and locked it. He climbed in beside his unintentional and accidental partner, concerned about her safety, but actually pleased with her company, as well.

"Where to?" The driver could care less if the greatest king was sitting in his taxi.

"The bridge."

The driver grunted for being asked to drive to such an inaccessible place. Charu and Sagar looked at each other… both had so many questions. But those questions could wait. It was clear to both of them that they had the same agenda, and therefore, the same destination. Sagar inched his fingers close to those of Charu's and touched them. When she did not move her hand away, he dared to cover it with his. The touch was full of reassurance of trust and friendship and confidence in each other. And though it seemed innocent and platonic, neither could ignore the undercurrent of something more…

CHAPTER TWENTY -FIVE

The freedom of Mortals

The village had rearranged itself again, around the Lord's house. It was the auspicious occasion of Maha Shiv Ratri and the villagers were sure that the Lord would make his appearance today without fail. People had gathered in throngs. The veranda had been filled up to its maximum capacity a long time ago. The people elbowing and jostling each other were struggling to keep ground. Nobody dared to sit or fall down, because they were sure to be mauled to death by the crazy stampede which was inevitable any moment. The wish of the people drunk on the power of God-men and superstitions was stronger than the fear of a gristly death.

A thick golden chain had been stretched between two wrought iron hooks in front of the main door to keep the toppling over enthusiastic devotees from breaching the privacy and sanctity of the fabled Lord. Recently, the Lord had started to sit in the hall on a marble throne engraved with real gold flowers. It had become too difficult to negotiate his way amidst sweaty and stinking bodies, uttering words of endearment. Some of them, encouraged by the faux concern showed by him, had decided that it was okay to throw themselves on him. It had occurred to the Lord, at times such as those, that how easy it would be for someone to just jab a dragger in his chest and escape in the sea of people. This fear had crept up due to the recent death of the henchman and the rumored escape of Phooli's husband.

His trepidation was at its apex. Looking at the endless line of people gathered from all over the state from his window, he had toyed with the idea of cancelling today's appearance. A cancellation meant a loss of crores of rupees which were normally collected on each occasion, in currency notes, cheques, and solid gold ornaments. Therefore, it was out of question. The passports had been stamped with the visiting visas and the troupes of mules were destined to travel in a week's time.

Again, his eyes averted to the solitary passport left behind. The owner, dead and therefore useless, had been one of his favorite. Again, her image clad in the red saree he had got her came back to him. When she had gone missing, unlike Phooli, he was sure that it had something to do with the child she had insisted on keeping, even in the face of dire consequences. She had hinted at going public, if her child was harmed. The Lord drunk on his own power had committed the gravest mistake of stepping into prohibited areas… but hadn't she been equally responsible? But in the end that did not matter. Sure, the boss had promised and the word was kept.

The Lord, knowing better than to ask the boss about her whereabouts, and thereby almost confirming his involvement with her and her pregnancy, kept mum. But he was sure, that the boss knew all about it; otherwise, there was no reason for the boss to send him the message to be on the lookout for a woman in red and yellow; the saree… nothing escaped the boss. In fact, the Lord feared that the boss had a hand in her murder, and soon he shall be paying with the same consequences. The day he had seen the body in the dingy, he was petrified. He had decided to keep pretending that he had nothing to do with the pregnancy. His pathetic efforts had only enraged the boss. He had promised not to make any more mistakes, and ran back to his den, keeping an unusually low profile.

The Lord looked at the swarming crowd with growing dislike and irk. To him, every young man looked like Ratan Macchi. He had been unable to rest properly since Ratan went missing, expecting him to turn up anywhere and everywhere. Every sound and every look seemed like a threat to him. The Lord stretched his hands in front of him, and looked at the uncontrollable tremor. A tremulous hand could not be raised in blessings or acknowledgement. There was a knock on his door and one of his guards spoke through the crack of the door, reminding him that it was time for his appearance.

The Lord shouted his affirmation and dismissed the guard. The usual ensemble of white and gold thread embroidered clothes was placed out on his bed. The nine rings which he used to wear, signifying each of the planets, had been polished to perfection and arranged in ascending order of their sizes. Many additional gold bracelets had found their way in his already enormous collection. The headband, with the peacock feather arranged on it, suddenly felt childish and absurd.

The Lord wore his gear. He picked up the red vermilion mixed with sandalwood oil and attempted to draw the tilak on his forehead. His shaking hands fell short of their job, and a stray line maligned his forehead. Cursing to himself, he attempted to remove the sticky red stain, which, as a result of some vigorous rubs, spread all over his forehead. His mounting frustration was not helping him either. He went to his cupboard and pulled out a vial half full of cocaine. He decided that a pinch of it would do the trick. He rejected the option of alcohol to that of the powder. He could not afford to go drunk and reeking of alcohol in front of the people. He measured out three lines on the table and snorted all of them in quick successions. The drug hit the top of his head and under a minute his tremors disappeared along with the overwhelming unease in his chest. He surveyed himself again in the mirror. His confidence, restored, made him dip three fingers in the red paste and pull three parallel lines on his forehead. There….now it was more like it. He perched the crown on his head at a becoming angle and was ready to be the Lord once again.

He opened the door with a push and meandered towards the ornate stairs. Below, his throne had been already placed and a tray fashioned to resemble a lotus was waiting at its feet, filled up to the brim with rose water and petals. Someone handed out the garland made of roses which he put around his neck. The guards fell in behind him, armed with loaded guns.

Today, being a very special day, the Lord had expected a large gathering, and therefore requested the boss for an extra guard. Seeing that his request had not been heeded, the Lord, his head buzzing with the drug induced temporary confidence and euphoria, had just thrown his head back and laughed out loud. This was ridiculous, his fear, that is… who could possibly harm him in front of this huge crowd of stupid devotees. The guns, loaded and ready for use, were comforting. The guards, with their budging muscles and fierce no nonsense attitude, exhaled safety. He started his descend after a dramatic pause at the top of the steps. The crowd went berserk. Chants of Hare Rama, Hare Krishna, echoed in the hall. The people, less fortunate and who were standing outside were brought to attention by the sudden uproar of those inside the perimeters.

As the Lord descended each step, the crowd went crazier and louder. With his hands poised in front of him, now unflinching and steady on the crutches of cocaine, he continued coming down, hovering his feet in air for a minute before stepping on the next one, his trail of white muslin following in wake. The people were bustling and pushing against the chain which creaked under pressure. Their impatience and asininity to meet their Messiah was like a soothing liniment to his bruised ego.

The marble floors had been polished until they shone. The servants always used a soapy water to clean it to perfection. It had to be an accident when the Lord's foot fell on a spot the servant had missed. Lord Dhayanand slipped and the small of his neck hit the step. The guards behind him reflexively caught the flowing trail which came off in their hands, being loosely attached to the main attire. The sound of the neck cracking was heard only by the Lord himself.

As he lay there on the landing of the steps unable to move or breath, his muddled mind couldn't even react with shock or the absurdity of dying in such a way. Before the rapidly ascending coldness of his limbs caught up with that of his slowing heart, his eyes were drawn to a man standing in the crowd, neither chanting nor shouting but looking directly at him. Dressed in the red and black of the household staff, the dusky tall youth was watching him intently. The Lord wanted to point at him so that he could be picked up from the maddening crowd, but his body refused to follow any of his orders. The last thing the dying eyes registered was the chain being unhinged from the strained hooks by the same youth who had haunted him since Phooli's death.

The sea of human feet, unable to discriminate between their God-man and other civilians, trampled whatever came its way. Before they could hold themselves back, the sheer number of bodies pressing each other had gained such an unstoppable momentum, that it was not until they had exhausted their energy, none of them realized that the uneven ground they were standing on was nothing but broken bones and sheared flesh. Among the twelve people who had died, the villagers were melancholic when they came to know, that the Lord was one of them. It had taken some effort from the police and cleaners to identify the pulped up body of the God-man. In death, the larger-than-life man appeared uncharacteristically small and common.

****

PI Gaurang knew what he would find in the house. He also knew that the death of one of the mule handlers just before the date of departure was bound to cause unpleasant ripples. He toyed with the idea of calling the boss, but then he let it go. He was sure the news must have reached the boss well before he was informed. As such, he wasn't too keen on letting the boss know that he was also planning to make himself scarce from the hippodrome.

The cold and calculative way in which the boss operated was become quiet inordinate for him. He was getting tired of playing the old game of Surplus killing. It was obvious that the boss felt no qualms regarding the number of people that had been killed in the last five years since the village had been picked up as the center. Like a power-crazed orca, the boss had probably started enjoying the highs of killing.

The PI sealed the house and walked up to the prayer room alone. Without the presiding Lord, the place looked shrunken and deflated. The scattered pillows covered in bright silk covers looked amiss and unbecoming. The white and maroon velvet curtains had been closed, throwing the room in a paradox of peace and serenity. PI Gaurang huffed and set out to work. He had to clear the whole house of all traces and evidences of drug peddling and prostitution, before the Crime Branch took over.

With the death of someone with a social strata as high as the Lord, it was only a matter of time. He also knew that the Crime Branch would not take very long to tighten the noose around his neck. As he collected the stash of cocaine pellets and syringes in a bag, he mulled over his recent predicament. He had to make his escape, if he wanted to live on the money he had accumulated in the last years. The momentary respite of a carefree future with his wife and unborn child, cheered him. His mind eased as he went through his plan. The prospect of hoodwinking the boss made him cocky and his gait jaunty. As the weight of the bag in his hand increased, a new outrageous idea hit him. He realized that he was carfyjng drugs worth a lot of money. Who is to know about this booty? As such, it could go off record. A smiled lit up his pensive face as he started focusing on laying his hands on every last bit of the white gold.

CHAPTER TWENTY-SIX

The Beginning of the Crusade

Ratan had anticipated a closure. He had been convinced that the raging fire in his heart, the amalgamation of sorrow and guilt would lift its weight off him if he could be instrumental in making the Lord meet his fate. As he stood at the threshold, with the myriad of people lashing at his back, eager to throw him away and reach their Lord, all he could feel was emptiness. The Lord, humanized in his final hour of death by being killed just like any other being, was just a very small replaceable part of a bigger mechanism. Ratan realized at that moment, that there were innumerable Phooli's and others trapped in the prison of poverty, which caters to no God, other than hunger.

As the Lord looked up at Ratan in his final moments, there was only the naked fear in his eyes. He did not want to die… not like that. Ratan, nauseated at the belittling of someone who had been the epitome of austerity for the simple people, under whose feet the same person was being crushed alive, moved aside to allow the crowd to break in. He removed his red turban and vest and threw it aside. The bloodied bandage, covering his midriff was already a nasty shade of rust. The fresh rush of shivers down his spine had nothing to do with excitement… Ratan realized that a fever was forming itself in his injured kidney. He could feel the toxin seep into his blood, slowly poisoning him.

By the time he had made his way all through the crowd, he was shaking uncontrollably, his body ablaze and his eyes glassy. He lost all sense of direction and purpose, as the last of his forced energy ebbed away. The road ahead seemed vaguely similar, and so Ratan trudged along; the pain in his loins increasing in crescendo, beating out all the sense of time and place with each painful throb. Finally, when his weakened body could not bear the trek anymore, Ratan kneeled over, the world turning into a confusing but wonderful kaleidoscope of colors.

****

The doctor was not yet in. She was never in, it seemed. All she was ever interested in was an autopsy. The nurse did not mind that. She had found the new doctor a poor replacement for the previous one. Not only was she seriously backdated in her approach, but absurd to the point where the old nurse had started questioning the authenticity of her degree. But who was she to complain or talk about genuine certificates. Half of the bureaucracy was running on excellently forged documents. When people deciding the budget of the country and safety standards of roads and bridges were thriving on such papers, what more harm could a silly girl pretending to play doctor do?

The nurse sighed as she saw a small rickshaw making its way towards the PHC. She could make out the floppy hand of a grown up man sticking out from the back seat. As the vehicle came closer, she went out to have a better look. The slate gray color of the skin of the young man's face was unmistakably that of someone very close to dead. As he was carried out from the seat, the nurse could make out that he was barely alive. She asked the men to leave him on one of the iron beds in the PHC, as she made her way to the telephone, intending to call the doctor, hoping in vain that the girl would know at least enough medicine to ease the dying man's pain.

As the men lay him on the bed, the old nurse took a good look at the young man's profile. It had been years since she had seen him, but in spite of the boy having filled out in a young man's body, the nurse recognized Ratan. Suddenly two absolutely unrelated events connected abruptly in her mind. Why on earth was she thinking of Constable

Tatya at that moment? She reasoned that it might have something to do with the same kind of extreme illness that both of them had been brought here. But she knew that was not it. She had heard something about Ratan losing his young wife Phooli after a short period of some curious illness. She was frustrated when she tried to recollect how the deceased looked, but her mind kept rerouting her to the hanging body of another young woman.

The phone's receiver clanked on the floor, the dial tone buzzing at a lazy hum. Something Tatya had said in fever induced confusion tapped the nurse roughly on her temple. Of course…Kasturi was murdered. The nurse automatically walked to the sick man and stick in a needle in his collapsed vein. She checked the temperature and administered the basic medicines to ease the fever. The nurse watched as the saline made its way in rapid drops into the man's body, bringing back some color to the ghastly white hands. She removed the soiled clumsily wrapped bandage and surveyed the wound.

Her experienced eyes, better than any degree education, knew at once that it was a stab wound which had probably injured a vital organ. Assault, murder, deaths, alleged suicides… and disappearances… these were way too much drama to be circumstantial and coincidental. Also, the appearance of this novice doctor, just in the midst of all these, stuck out like a sore thumb. Some instinct borne out of being in the medical field for decades, told the nurse to not inform the doctor about Ratan. Silently, she removed the locks at the legs of the bed and wheeled the man down the corridor and into a small dark room, which doubled as the morgue. She was glad that the clinic was practically empty and there was no one about. Then, she took a white sheet and covered the barely moving man from head to toe, adjusting it around his legs to resemble a dead body.

She knew that the fake doctor, whatever her agenda was, would have no reason to visit the gloomy and stinking morgue. For now, the nurse reasoned, that it was the best chance Ratan had to stay alive, lying amidst the dead. Adjusting the medicines and fluids in various different cannulas, the nurse locked the door and made way to her quarters.

She could not risk to be seen in the PHC today. She knew that by being away, she would most probably be saving the young man's life as well as hers.

****

Revathi studied the minute black and white negatives against the torch light. The blurry pictures looked like a gathering of people in a party. A collage of people with as yet hidden identities, just a swab away was making no sense to the reporter. She as well might have romanticized the whole thing in her head; but in the era of cellphones, the art of clicking away on a not so conspicuous camera with a film seemed almost paleontological. Frustrated, she rolled the film back into its dark cocoon. Her stomach rumbled loudly, reminding her that she was on her last bit of ration and soon, she will be forced to go out into the open if she was considering surviving. She rolled herself on the floor of the van, in an attempt to keep hunger at bay for some more time.

Her mind wandered to the day Sagar had risked his life, to send her the photographs. She had suggested a meeting in her office. But lately, the doctor had become progressively paranoid about something. This time too, when he had called her out of nowhere, he had sounded frightened. He had agreed to see her in the press, but later, he had used the 'code'. Even that was his idea. The whimsical sounding thing sounded like a brainchild of a hyper-suspicious mind. Sometimes she had wondered whether the doctor was a little crazy and whether she should be taking him seriously. But the recent turn of events had added up to the conclusion that the doctor had all the reasons to be on his guard.

Revathi knew that the undeveloped pictures had no story to say until developed. Also, she seemed to be missing a part of the story here. Sagar's intentional mention of the news related to her father's death could not be gratuitous. But how could a seemingly unrelated event be related to the current deaths?

Something clanked loudly on the rusted door of the van. Revathi's senses, heightened by hunger and fear, made her pick up an iron shovel kept at the corner of the van, and position herself just below the front window. She crouched low, her ears rigged up to pick up the earliest sign of threat. She held her breath… who could it be? Who else knew about this place? Her eyes were fixed at the small part of the tinted window wherein the film had peeled off. The moonlight was streaming through the gap making her feel like a trapped animal. Suddenly, she could see a shadow cross the van. Revathi, too frightened to even breath, found the effort compressing her chest. Her heart was pounding vigorously, expecting the flimsy door to be kicked in at any moment. Instead, there was a sharp but short rap on the window pane, followed by a soft female voice calling out. Relief flushed over Revathi.

Quickly, she opened the door and let in the two huddled dark shadows into the van. It was clear from her expression that Revathi hadn't expected to see the doctor alive ever again. She ran up to him and hugged him tightly, dissolving into sobs of relief; and Sagar, just happy to be alive, hugged back. Charu stood a little at the side, her feet making to and fro movements, etching straight lines on the dirt. The sudden expression of what seemed like love between Sagar and Revathi irked her. But what else had she expected? She collected her thoughts and put the misplaced emotions in the back burner. They had very little time, because Charu knew, that the next consignment of the mules was to sail in three days.

When the initial excitement had subdued, Revathi decided to ask the big question. How on the earth did they know that she was here? The reaction of both the people was so starkly different, that Revathi had more questions than answers. Charu looked down, fidgeting with the edge of her saree, while Sagar looked at her with a sheepish smile.

"I followed you here on two accounts. I was intrigued to know where you used to disappear for days before any breaking news. Once, I thought that you had a rendezvous with someone in this most unlikely place. And the second time, I thought that you were having an affair. But then, I lost my phone signal within half a kilometer from your van, and I had read my share of mystery potpourris to realize that there was a jammer at work. So I added up…"

Revathi was looked owl eyed at his direction. The mousy doctor seemed to have the brain and heart of an elephant. Then something occurred to her.

"If you were sure about my hideout, why didn't you ask me to meet you here?"

Sagar did not speak for a moment, but when he answered, all the temporary mirth had evaded his face.

"I knew your phone was tapped. Asking you to come to the dirt road was just my feeble attempt to confirm my doubts. When you came there to apparently hoping to meet me, I had already had a visitor. I wanted to make sure, that my theory was right. I was sure that the police inspector knew every move I made. I also had a strong suspicion that he was just a pawn in this huge game of drug trafficking. I had a very good idea about who the person was, but I had to see for myself."

"And, did you see the person? Who was it?"

"I am not sure that's her real name, but I have heard someone calling her 'Mohini.'"

"Mohini?"

"Mohini!"

Charu started to fidget again. It was clear to her, that out of the trio she was the unintentional forerunner. She knew way much than either of the smarter ones. She had been a little put off when the doctor hadn't asked her how she knew where Revathi was. There was a sudden silence in the room as the conversation stopped. She looked up to find both of them looking at her with expectation. She had yet to say her part of the story. She knit her brows. Were these people really more educated than her? Wasn't it clear to them yet, how she knew, what she knew?

"Gaurang knew about your hideout. He had known about it for years now. Initially, he told me, that he had followed you here a few times… expecting to either catch you with someone, to create a scandal and later, just to look at you in your private moments. I don't think, he ever realized that he was actually trespassing the safe house. But then, the man has never been able to think beyond the length and breadth of his manhood. Many times, while, em… he was with me, he would boast about having a hold over you. That seemed to get him excited. The first day he let it out, I kept wondering why you needed to go there, in the first place. You don't know, but I have been following your articles regularly, after you wrote a piece about my sister…"

"Your sister?"

"Yes, Kasturi…."

"Oh…"

Revathi's stomach gave a lurch again. She coughed awkwardly to cover up her protesting stomach. Charu quickly reached inside her bundle and pulled out few sesame seed and jaggery sweets, rolled until the creaminess and the stickiness merged into a heavenly texture. Revathi was only too glad for the food and chomped off a couple of them in four bites.

"We have to hurry. The consignment ships out this Friday."

Again Charu was met with the same element of surprise and awe from both of them. An added glimmer of something like respect in the doctor's eyes made Charu's heart skip in joy. Suddenly she was filled up with more courage than ever, for the event she had for years been preparing herself.

"I know, because, I am one of the twenty-four women finalized to leave… twenty-three, that is, after Ganga died."

"Ganga? Who is she?"

Charu was really surprised now. How could people be so ill prepared before jumping into something as intricate and detailed as this syndicate? Was it even possible to get so far, without knowing anything about Ganga? After all, she was the reason why the women had been rounded up in a hurry, and the boss had decided to round up the headquarters from the village. In a way, Ganga had been the catalyst instrumental in the slow but sure crumble of the drug concrete that had been living in each house, each lane and each family in the village.

"You mean, you don't know who Ganga was? Did you not realize who she was, when you were dissecting her body?" Sagar was unprepared for this volley of questions. A look at Revathi confirmed that they were unable to see something which was supposed to be so obvious, that it was staring them right at their face. Sagar went through steps of the last autopsy in his mind. Had there been something which he had missed? He thought about the fetus, in approximately 26-27 weeks of gestation. He urged his mind to go through the chopped off fingers and the missing half of the face… and his thoughts fixed themselves on the gold toe rings. Hadn't he had an idea about them? Something about women not wearing gold on their feet commonly, except those from affluent families.

Charu was sitting between Revathi and Sagar, her feet drawn up to her chest and her arms encircling them with her hands forming a clasp. Her face, unnaturally young and childlike, without the extensive make-up, was resting on her knees. She sighed…. It was time for her to tell them a story. Who was Ganga? The answer was not a simple introduction, but demanded a story… a full one, without which, understanding her and her sacrifice would not be possible.

CHAPTER TWENTY-SEVEN

The Sting of Fate

Uma felt hot. The sun was unusually harsh. For the first time in two months, she acknowledged the absurdity of having the working area on the top floor, covered entirely with glass. With Nargis absent for last ten days, supposedly engaged in her daughter's marriage, the sorting had come up on her head. The free flow of food and water had been suddenly rationed. Also, the rest of the women, though never overtly hostile were nothing more than believers of peaceful coexistence.

With Nargis gone, there was no one who cared to see if she was ok. The only warmth she felt coming to her was from the supervisor, surprisingly. But she rarely made it obvious in front of others. Breaking the first image of a stern, grumpy, and rude person, the supervisor had been extremely helpful and exclusive regarding her. She had been kind to introduce her name to a drug company which was recruiting young men and women in a harmless trial.

The supervisor has said she had chosen Uma because of her simplicity, dedication, and poverty. She had sternly asked her not to discuss any of it with anyone, least the people working with her, or else there was a very valid chance that she might lose the unique opportunity. The sum assured to her was more than enough to buy years of silence and loyalty.

The supervisor had convinced her that the medicine in question was a very nourishing vitamin indeed and had no negative side effects. So persuasive was her speech that Uma decided that it was okay to be silent on the small detail regarding her missed periods. She had been three weeks overdue and had not really thought about it until her mother-in-law, curious as to her regular visits to the temple without the customary monthly periodic breaks, was immediately wise to the happenings.

The news of an imminent addition to the household was taken with joy and a tinge of jealousy. The elder daughter in law, yet to bear a child, was suddenly geared into action, fearing the birth of her brother-in-law's son prior to hers, and thereby becoming the rightful owner of his grandfather's property. Uma, oblivious to all the family politics she had instigated, was busy day dreaming about the money she was going to get from her job in the factory, and also from the miracle medicine factory. She dreamt of buying a real silk saree with real gold thread work. She wanted to buy a pair of gold buttons for Mahesh to replace the fake ones he was gifted by her father. The possibilities were endless. She imagined a beautiful world waiting for her child and she couldn't wait!

Mahesh was out in the heart of the sea when Uma was introduced to the trial. The daily struggle to survive the tumulus sea, and attempt to gather her fruits from the depths of her womb, became a daily adventure. As the onboard water tanks started filling up with pound lobsters and red sea urchins, the general mood became buoyant and cheerful. Nothing cheers up the poor like the prospect of good business. Mahesh entered his logs with the quantity of his catches. Although humble in comparison to his much more experienced partners, he had had a decent haul.

At the end of the day, as the men opened their ration of toddy and drank themselves to oblivion, Mahesh found his heart turn fondler for his young feisty wife with an unmatched appetite for life and adventure. When he had left for the five day fishing spree, she had given him a tearful farewell. He had not anticipated such a heart-wrenching experience. As she had clung to his shirt, her face buried in the hairs on his chest, he had felt his heart break. He had caressed the stump of clump of hair which had grown into oddly beautiful curls.

Back here on the rocking boat, Mahesh suddenly remembered something. He touched his pocket and removed a small copper box decorated with plastic gems. He had bought it a couple of years back from the village fair. He looked around to make sure no one was around. Any show of vulnerability would undoubtedly draw sneer and ridicule from the rough crowd, he knew. The distant sound of drunken laughter and vulgar jokes confirmed that the men were lost in their own world. Slowly, Mahesh opened the box and brought it near his face, taking a lung full of fragrance emaciating from it. He pulled out a coil of dark coiled bunch of hair and touched it to his face.

Unknown to his wife, he had picked up the lock she had sheared off and kept it with himself for safe keeping. The mingle of jasmine, coconut, and an earthy smell of clay clung to the lock and for a moment Mahesh felt his wife, Uma.

Strangely, he still felt a high sense of insecurity creeping on his mind; the same insecurity and discomfort that he had felt in the factory. For some reason, his mind took him back to the spotlessly white walls and the family photographs hanging on them, and the sandalwood shavings garlands on each sans one… the up turned face of the laughing girl, forgotten intentionally, as if being punished even in death. Mahesh was reminded of the artificial lawns and the waning image of the island as his dingy had pulled back… The single un-garlanded photograph on the wall kept demanding his mind's attention. The woman trapped in the frame was smiling and coaxing him to figure out something very important. Mahesh knew he had to be on land as soon as he could.

****

Lata eyed her husband with a mixture of disbelief, fear, and awe. His recent devotion, adoration, and care, had confused her. Her body and mind, tuned to abuse and shame, found this sudden ounce of kindness and respect disturbing and alluring in equal measures. She knew that it might have something to do with the child growing in her womb. She knew that her husband, an orphan brought up by an abusive uncle, having learnt that bullying and snatching were the only ways in life, had gone so far on the roads of sin that coming back, or taking a detour, was not only difficult, but seemingly impossible.

So, that day, when Gaurang appeared on the door steps, with the crazed look of a cornered animal, with a heavy bag embossed with the well-known emblem of the Lord: the rose, Lata feared the worst. Gaurang had flung the bag on the nearby chair and removed his soaking wet shirt. The fan, pushed to its top speed limit was finding it difficult to keep up with the anxious and worked up inspector. Lata, unsure of how he might react, was still walking on egg shells around him. Silently she fetched him some water and waited for his order. Gaurang was strangely pensive and silent. There was neither sneer nor harsh words for his wife. Rather, he surprised her by holding her hand gently while returning the empty glass.

Lata, unaccustomed to his gentleness couldn't help her tears; and the glass slipped off her shaking hands. Gaurang stood up, and reflexively, Lata cringed her eyes and cowered, turning her face away, and expecting a slap. But what came next hurt her yet more. A defeated man, finally caught up by his past and stronger demons, was holding her with her shoulders. His head hung up, and his body trembling with shame, at the effect he had on his wife, Gaurang was doing the unthinkable. In words unsaid, he asked for forgiveness from his wife and hoped that this small repentance might help him make things a little better for his unborn child.

Lata's kind heart forgave readily. She hugged her husband as an equal for the first time since her marriage, and passed on as much unconditional love and comfort as she could muster. After a while, when Gaurang had regained some of his composure, Lata asked him to sit on the bed while she sat beside him. She hadn't asked him anything about the suspicious looking bag, and Gaurang knew she wouldn't. He had no intension of pulling her into it either; the less she knew, the better. Suddenly he realized just how tired he was. He shifted his position and laid his head on her lap. After an initial hesitation, Lata ran her fingers lovingly through his hair, tugging it occasionally to give him a soothing massage. Before long, Gaurang had drifted off to sleep. There was, in fact, a detour, in the road of life: a choice… at each and every step; and he had taken his.

CHAPTER TWENTY-EIGHT

Death is stealthy

The passport office was practically empty. This time of the year, it was a lull period, with job opportunities at their lowest and the weather way too hot to be travelling; But for a sleepy little city such as the one nearest to the fishermen's village, slow and lackluster. Uma held her scanty certificates tightly in her hands, the sweat seeping through the flimsy paper leaving black-brown smudgy fingerprints on them. The man who had accompanied her to the office was a stranger. She had never seen him before. He was burly and towered well a hand above her head. It seemed as if he could easily take her whole head in one of her hands and crack it open with a flick of his wrist. Thick cords of blood vessels throbbed like snakes on his neck.

Uma did not appreciate her companion as soon as she realized that he lacked basic education as well as etiquette. The supervisor madam had promised Uma to accompany her herself, but on the said day, she had excused herself, citing an unplanned meeting with the owner of the factory, Keva Devi. The man happened to be present right there conveniently, and was thereby sent along with Uma to the passport office.

Uma had oiled her hair and parted it on her right, adorning her forehead with the special sparkling re-orange vermilion she had bought from the fair. A loop of freshly bloomed jasmine ran around her opulent bun and peeked above her head, framing her small face in a white fragrant halo. Her large eyes, naturally dark with extra-long lashes shone with the sparkle of adventure.

Things had been like a dream, since she had been enrolled in the medicine program. Within a week, the supervisor had given her the excellent news that she had been handpicked along with a few other precious girls to go abroad in the coming months as representatives of the company. Again, Uma thought better of mentioning her pregnancy to the supervisor. The prospects of putting her feet on foreign land had made her euphoric.

The phone given by Nargis lay forgotten and discharged in same dreamlike state. Uma literally flew into the new world where everything was much more colorful, promising, and full of gaiety. The medicine stock given to her had to be taken strictly as per prescription; but she found the effects so pleasing and comforting that she sneaked in an extra dose and continued to do so when she failed to notice any obvious side effects. She believed that the nourishing vitamin was helping her child grow. After all, anything which made her feel so happy had to be a medical miracle.

Mahesh had been home for a couple of weeks and had been relieved to find his fears unfounded and baseless. Her new found passion for work and new ventures for extra income were great news and welcome. What made him slightly uncomfortable was the news of her pregnancy. Indeed he was thrilled about it, but the news came from his mother, rather than from his wife. When confronted, Uma had laughed it off, saying that it hardly mattered as to who was the bearer of the news. The laugh seemed pressed and mechanical. To Mahesh, it sounded as if Uma was having second thoughts about her pregnancy.

The changes were always there, Mahesh would say, if asked. They were subtle, and all the family members seemed to attribute the eccentricities to her initial stages of pregnancies, and her inherited child-like attitude; but her faltering sense of neatness and personal hygiene were red flags. This was something Mahesh had seen earlier in someone he had known as a child and grown up with. That, the same vice had found its way into his life was unfathomable for him.

How had something like this even happened? He asked Uma, but she refused vehemently. Even the idea of taking drugs was abhorred by her. All she took were her daily prescribed medicines for the trial. When Mahesh demanded to see them, Uma broke down complaining about the medical company which had withdrawn the trial suddenly, without any explanation.

Mahesh tried to comfort his hysterical wife promising to do everything in his power to help her. Uma, her eyes hollowed and skin drawn tight over her jutting bones smiled suddenly at him and for a second, Mahesh could see his innocent wife peeking from behind this person whom he did not know. When she clasped the lapels of his shirt and asked him in hushed notes if he really meant it, Mahesh realized that he had already lost his beloved wife.

His premonition on the boat had come true. The thin skeletal arms sticking out of the oversized blouse were holding him with astounding strength. The slight budge of her stomach just above her pubis was the only remaining curve on her once voluptuous body. A quiver on the budge saddened Mahesh further as he knew that it was only a matter of time, before he would lose all that he had ever valued in life.

Uma, realizing that Mahesh was impotent, as far as his promise of doing everything in his power was concerned, slowly released her grip, her smile retreating along with the momentary flicker of hope. She slowly stepped back and made a mad dash towards the door, screaming like a wounded animal. She slammed her body on the shut door again and again, trying to bend it outwards to create a gap big enough to hinge her finger in it and price it open.

The door rattled and screeched but did not yield to her frail body. Mahesh, helpless with love and a broken heart could do nothing other than stand and watch. Afraid that she might hurt herself grievously, Mahesh positioned himself between her and the door. Overcome with fatigue and weakness, Uma slumped in his arms, her body swat in perspiration and her lips cracked and parched.

Mahesh carried her to the bed, the same on which, on the very first night his nubile but lively wife had shown him just what a woman could do; the same place, where he had learnt the difference between love and lust and the beauty of the former. With tears, blurring his eyes, he put a pillow below her head and tied her hands and feet to the posts. He had hammered extra nails in the headrests to make them sturdy. He knew, that the lack of drug would wake her up sooner or later and make her body cringe and beg till she had no more energy or life left in her.

He picked up the small bag Uma used to carry to work. He was going through it hoping to find some clues which would help him. Another man in his place would have gathered a crowd and faced the supervisor who was obviously the culprit. But Mahesh had always lacked the spirit. He cursed himself for being a coward and not being able to stand up for his wife. More tears stung his eyes as he struggled to look at the nick-knacks in the bag.

There were a couple of beautifully colored conches, small and dainty, which had been pierced and tied together with a piece of black string. Mahesh realized that in better days, Uma must have snuck in the souvenirs to make a medallion for her child, a child who in probability would not see the daylight ever in his life. He inverted the whole bag on the cot and the rest of the contents dropped down. A small rectangular object caught his eye. On closer inspection, he realized that it was a phone. His curiosity was annexed. Neither he, nor his wife had ever owned a phone. He pushed the buttons and realized that it was dead. He felt urged to find a charger immediately.

A quick search in the house yielded none which matched the make of the phone. After asking his mother to look after his confined wife, Mahesh ran outside his house in search of a charger. He knew that the tea shop had a multi-charger which could cater to many different types of phones at once. He ran all the distance and found the place virtually empty. He looked about frantically, trying to locate the tell-tale white cable. For a split second he thought that the owner had had it removed. But then, right behind the counter was the charger. Mahesh plugged it in and waited for the equipment to come alive. What he was expecting, he did not know. He did not have the faintest idea as to where it had come from either. But if it was amongst Uma's things, there was a high chance that this alien object had something to do with her present condition. He picked up the phone, but it had hardly charged beyond a percent and therefore refused to get switched on.

A few customers came in for some tea and idle banter. They threw casual looks in his direction, which to Mahesh looked menacing and convicting. For him, it seemed that everyone in the village knew about his wife. He bowed his head and placed it on the counter top, less in order to rest, and more to hide his face. He tried to dissect his feelings. He was sure he knew most of the answer he sought, and it made him feel guilty. He should have been filled with bitterness and vengeance. But instead, like a coward, he was trying to tie up and hide his innocent wife, ready to sacrifice her and his unborn child on the alter in order to protect his hollow honour.

A sharp succession of rings jarred his chain of thoughts and self-reproach. Although no one in particular had even noticed the ring; for Mahesh, it felt like all the conversations in the room had stopped, and everyone was looking at him. He snatched the phone and ran out of the shop, the back of his neck blushing in self-consciousness.

A number was flashing on the screen. Green and red icons were blinking simultaneously. Mahesh was surprised at the promptness of the call. How on earth had the person on the other end known that the phone had been switched on? Then again, he was not the sharpest needle in the stack and decided not to give the matter anymore thought. He gathered his small ration of courage, and pressed the green button and put the phone to his ear.

There was a woman on the other end, and she sounded worried and sad that it was the husband and not Uma herself who had picked up the phone. Mahesh was further surprised when she knew exactly what had happened to her, and found his suspicions growing uncomfortably fast against this anonymous caller. When asked, she introduced herself as Nargis. She asked about Uma's condition, and whether a doctor had been involved.

Mahesh's skepticism about the woman could not hold him back from breaking into uncontrollable sobs when he told Nargis that she was 14 weeks pregnant and possibly not going to survive.

What Nargis told Mahesh over the next ten minutes, before the batteries ran out again, made Mahesh's already depleted store of courage run dry. What she was suggesting was preposterous and in Mahesh's opinion, might not be even called for. The whole idea was larger than life, and he was sure that there had to be some other way involving easier and less risky methods. Nargis seemed to have known that she was talking to an extremely thick headed man and who would not know what to do until Uma was taken and returned dead after she had served the money's worth. So, she had told Mahesh just exactly what was going to happen that very day. A lack of reply from him confirmed the worst to Nargis, before the phone died.

Mahesh looked at the blank screen. He was actually relieved that the conversation had been cut short. The conversation was making him uncomfortable and increasingly inadequate. What was asked of him was so big a feat that even thinking about it made him sick. Was he ready to take such an unnecessary step? Or was it the only step that he could take? He returned the phone back in his pocket, vowing never to use it again. Nargis could keep her thrilling feature films to herself. He would just keep his wife to himself and comfort her in her last hours.

He knew the end was near because that is how he had seen Kasturi behave before she got a little better only to be… found dead. She did not die naturally; Nargis's voice seemed to be screaming in Mahesh's head. He clasped his hands over his ears and walked rapidly towards his house. He had heard enough. He had seen enough. Things would take their own course just as destined. The image of his dying wife floated in front of his eyes, and he shut them to drive it away. Then, just as he thought that he had succeeded, the image took its place as one of the framed pictures on the factory's white wall.

CHAPTER TWENTY-NINE

Mohini

There were no more possible twists and turns possible in this one night, Revathi thought. The discovery of the long lost Kodak reel, the sudden mysterious appearance of Sagar and Charu, the general agreement of an unknown and very dangerous mastermind behind the drug kingdom of the West, and now, the enigma around someone called Ganga, who, according to Charu, was the reason why everything started, and the very reason everything would end.

She fished out a jumbo sized tube of mosquito repellant and squeezed out some and rubbed in all over her arms and legs. The doctor's eyes followed subconsciously. Revathi caught the glimmer of anger and hurt pass through Charu's eyes and was amused. She tossed the tube to Charu who caught it without a smile debating whether to throw it back at her face rudely or decline sardonically. She did none because the mosquitoes were having a gala buffet, and she sheepishly smeared her body with the cream, instantly experiencing relief. She passed on the tube to Sagar who had been trying to re-ignite the dwindling fire with his feet. Sagar looked at the tube and took it with his good hand, squeezing it awkwardly, spilling the contents all over himself. Charu looked at Revathi, expecting her to jump up to help him. Instead, she just curled her long dusky legs under her body and returned to her scrutiny of the reel.

The doctor cursed and decided that squeezing the medicine with the help of his mouth was a good option. Charu suppressed a smile and stretched out a hand towards him. Sagar leaned over and dropped the tube in her hand, inching closer to where she sat. Charu collected the spilled ointment and started to smear small quantities on his feet. Then she motioned him to pull up his sleeves as far as he could, which he did. She looked straight at his eyes while her fingers found the softer insides of his arms and wrists. She rubbed the cream in small circular movements and inched down crossing over to the back of the hand, never breaking contact. She got up and stood behind him. Sagar adjusted his glasses, relieved that the reflection of the fire had aptly hid his eyes from that of Revathi's. He was sure, that his sharp friend would have picked up his rising desire with just a look. Charu, her each touch making her blush as much as the doctor, gently pulled back the collar, and applied the cream on the smooth and cool skin like that of black marble. She ran light fingers over his neck and pushed her hands from his back onto his neck. As her hands crossed the nipples with the slightest of her touch, the doctor shivered involuntarily, which he tried to camouflage by trying to shake off a nonexistent insect. The whole act from a bystander's view was innocent and ordinary. Yet, the undercurrent was so palpable, that Revathi decided to cough loudly in order to make her presence felt. She would have been more than happy to play cupid, but for now, the writer in her was somersaulting and doing headstands to stop itself from killing these two love birds.

The charm broken crudely by the purposeful hacking coughs left Charu and Sagar extremely shy and not strangely breathless, considering that neither had remembered to breathe in the last two minutes. Revathi fished out a cigarette and lit it as she laid down on her sleeping bag. She looked at Charu, offering her a drag which she declined. The doctor, she knew, did not smoke. Revathi could take it no more. She inhaled a long drag and looked at Charu again.

"So, who was she, Charu? Who was Ganga?"

"She… she was the Bapat's daughter."

✶✶✶✶✶✶✶✶✶✶✶✶✶

Ratan was blinking rapidly. He could hardly believe that he was looking at a real bird. Initially, he was certain that the robin sitting on the netted window was just an illusion, a shape-shifter and would soon dissolve into thin air. When it flew away and did not come back for a very long time, his fears were confirmed. He turned his head to take an account of his surroundings. He was a little disheartened to find heaven in shambles. Or perhaps his recent deeds had landed him in hell? He gulped down some saliva, and was surprised to find that there was no thirst. He was feeling better than ever actually. Even the pain on the left side of his abdomen had reduced to a mild throb. He turned his head towards the window again. The bird was back, dancing in circles, his red bottom exposed in the process, without doubt in the immediate presence of a duller female. The bird sang out in a melody which ended in an awkward quack and only then was Ratan convinced that he was not yet dead and he was still on planet earth.

He looked at his hands and feet and discovered that there were no lines attached to him. In fact, he was absolutely free. The door also seemed to be partially ajar. He was wearing a strange ensemble of purple pants and a pink top two sizes too big for him and strangely opened at the back. The crispness indicated that it was brand new and never used before. The emblem of the Government printed in blue ink on the clothes and on the sheets told him that he was in a civil establishment. Although he was grateful to his benefactors, he had no reason to stay on their hospitality anymore. He had to move on. There was nothing more for him in this village… every nook and corner re-minded him painfully of his Phooli.

He swung his legs off the bed and felt the cold hard floor under his feet. He stood up gingerly, expecting to double up with pain. But when nothing happened he was relieved. He looked about for something to put on his feet. When he found nothing he decided that it would do and walked bare foot towards the door. A babble of voices just across the veranda reached his ears as he was about to test the door. Some-thing in the cheerfulness of the voice cut through him like a stab of ice; a memory from a time long back from memory; a voice which had covered the deadly drugs in its honeycomb, and poured them down his throat; eroding his soul and his being. Ratan found an old fear rising back in his heart; a dark irrational fear which had been worse than death itself. But along with fear, there was a feeling of disbelief. He had seen with his own eyes, Keva Bai banishing Mohini from the factory. Later, it had also been fabled, that she had been killed. But there was no mistake that the person, donning the white apron and stethoscope, laughing her signature laugh was one and the same person.

Ratan knew that she was anything but a doctor. His cornered mind could only come to one conclusion. Her presence here, of all the places could only mean that she had come here to finish his story. He ducked behind the window and hazarded a peek just above the sill. It seemed that she was dilly-dallying with some poor sod that was apparently getting worse with the quack's medicine. The elderly nurse was standing at a little distance with a skeptical look on her face, her arms crossed tightly across her chest. Suddenly, the nurse looked right at his direction and he ducked just at the nick of time, unsure whether she had caught a glimpse of him or not.

The voices seemed to be coming closer. Ratan shrunk further and further in the corner, trying to hide himself amongst the debris and the general junk. There seemed to be some sort of argument going on between the two women. Ratan waited as their shadows passed across the window. The dangerously sweet voice of Mohini drifted through the window and froze Ratan's blood.

"Sister, why don't you care for your own old neck? I am the doctor. I know the medicines, see? Paracetamol, calpol, xyz, abc…." She ended with a sneer. The laugh in her words did not reach her eyes. Ratan, from his hiding place, could see the frail old nurse finally losing some of her courage and becoming a little unsure of herself. She stepped back, stuttering an apology and sounding distressed. Mohini, with a change in persona, apt for the stage, broke into one of her toothy smiles and held the shaking nurse by her shoulders.

"Sister! We are friends, are we not? I don't know why you choose not to believe me…. Now, what is this dump?"

Mohini kicked the door in. The moisture eaten door buckled under the assault falling with a resounding thud which reverberated through Ratan's being. He pushed himself further in the shadows, disturbing a cloud of dust covering the old forgotten furniture. The petite but surprisingly menacing woman, with her hands dipped deep in her aprons, her shoulders hunched comically, and a smile drawn sardonically on her face, entered the room and eyed the empty bed.

The nurse, petrified to silence followed her and let out a long sigh, in spite of herself when she saw the bed as well. Mohini smacked her lips, her eyes twitching with suppressed excitement. Ratan watched as she drew nearer to the bed, and ran her fingers over the sheets, lingering on the pillow. Suddenly she pulled her head back and sniffed deeply. Ratan could imagine her catching his trail like a blood hound. At any moment she would turn and walk up to him and tear his guts out…. Mohini breathed again, her eyes still closed as if in rapture.

"Ah… sister, the spring is here. Do you know, what reminds me of the spring? The smell of blood… the putrid smell of blood, spilt and forgotten to be cleaned…."

The traces of relief which had crept on the old nurse's face faltered. Mohini leaned her small angelic face obscenely near that of the nurse.

"Oh, nurse…did you not learn proper waste management in nursing school? Did you not learn that bleach must be used to neutralize the odor and the traces?"

The nurse's frail frame shook as she stepped back, stuttering her answer in a poor effort to hide her rising panic. As she inched back, she tripped on the broken door and fell down. Mohini changed her demur immediately, and her tone softened.

"Oh my God, sister. Are you hurt? Please, here, hold my hand. Let us get out of this awful place at once! And what is this smell? Maybe, a rat died here or something. I will ask Yadav to clean this place."

The nurse unsure about the abrupt sweetness and nonchalance did not know if she was being lured into a trap. She held back, motionless right where she had fallen down, ignoring the proffered hand. Mohini's smile disappeared and her face withdrew in an unsightly scorn. Ratan watched from the safety of his corner. He could see the old nurse heaving, beads of perspiration rolling down her temples.

After almost a minute she extended a shaky hand towards Mohini's and forced a smile in a feeble attempt to pacify the woman. Just as the nurse extended her hand, Mohini withdrew hers and straightened. With astonishing swiftness she encircled the old woman and yanked her by her bun. The frightened nurse screamed in pain. The crazy spark in Mohini's eyes was edging on being maniac. She pulled harder until the nurse's neck was exposed.

Then slowly, as if sitting down to examine a flowering plant, Mohini squatted on the broken door. The rotten wood didn't even creak. The sunlight beaming inside the room caught hold of something silvery in Mohini's hand. The nurse must have seen it too because the fear in her eyes had converted into pleas of life.

"Why is there a freshly made bed in the morgue sister? Why is there bloody bandage in the bin? Sister, am I not your friend? Who was here? The doctor? Was the doctor here?"

The cutter was inching deeper inside the chin with each question. When the nurse did not answer, Mohini suddenly started laughing and started to run the cutter rapidly down the throat. The old withered skin of the nurse was not as supple as she would have liked, but still the spurts of blood were fun to watch.

The hypodermic needle which hit her just between her neck and head felt like a joke to her initially. She half hoped to see an imbecile standing there poking a rod at her. The second stab in her left eye followed by four more repeated ones finally told Mohini that the third player was serious. Her injured eye failed to register her nemesis and she left the nurse to swing the lethal weapon at him. Only when Ratan, taller and stronger than Mohini caught her by her neck and picked her up to his own height so that she could see him directly into his eyes did she realize who he was.

The cutter cluttered harmlessly on the floor as the effect of the hypodermic at the back of the neck started taking action. Blood dropped from her left eye and a docile smile played on her lips, and for a second she resembled the Madonna. But Ratan could neither forget nor forgive the devil who had sacrificed thousands of his village people. He squeezed harder all the while keeping her face close to hers looking at her right pupil. Only when it dilated and stayed that way did he let go. Mohini fell down on the floor.

"Quick, take this damn door and put it back… just put it back."

Nurse had patched the 2 inch gash with a gauge and was again her old self. Ratan did as told. The pine door was ancient and moth-eaten. He picked it up and arranged it agreeably. The nurse quickly limped towards the fallen assassin and checked her vitals to make sure that she was indeed dead. Later, both of them sat on the rickety bed and thought about what had happened in the past twenty minutes… why had she thought that the doctor was back. And if she was hell bent on killing, who was she? To which, Ratan explained to the nurse who Mohini was. She was not surprised. Ratan also explained the circumstances in which he got stabbed, and because he felt that the nurse had saved his life, he also revealed how he had done away with the Lord. To his surprise, the nurse laughed and clapped his back.

"I knew you as a child. But I never knew you had so much in you. Well done my son. Now there is only one thing to do."

The truck leaving for the incinerator was due in a couple of hours. The patient-nurse duo took their time to roll the midget into a tight small ball good enough for an average garbage bag. They casually carried the bio-hazardous substance and disposed it off in the truck. It was a Friday and the nurse knew that all wastes were incinerated on that day. The compound was empty; and with no medical services, the PHC was in slumber.

CHAPTER THIRTY

Love always wins

Lata was shedding tears. Crying had become a part of her life. For years she had been waiting for this day… and the day came. Slowly she removed her husband's head from her lap and arranged it on the pillow comfortably. She arranged the blanket around his feet so that he would be comfortable. Slowly, so as not to disturb him, she moved out of the bed, and went to the small garden. The turmoil in her heart could only be calmed by her plants.

Earlier this morning she had received the call she had been dreading for the past few days since Ganga was found. The voice on the other end, calm and composed as ever was neither angry nor happy. Of course the news of the pregnancy had reached… what followed was a one sentence statement. Not a request. Not an order; a statement. Lata walked into her garden. The hibiscus and the roses were in bloom. The jasmines were scanty but enough to intoxicate the air. She took in a lung full of the fragrance and felt happy… almost looking forward to what was going to happen next.

Her abuse and pregnancy had left her physically weak. The voice on the phone knew. So there was a different plan… an easier way. She had forgotten why she had come to the garden. There were chores to be done. She could not while away her time. She walked inside her house and inside the room. Gaurang was asleep just as she had left him. She cleared the table noiselessly and folded his uniform, keeping it neatly inside the cupboard. Then she walked up to him and sat near his head and started caressing him… something which she had never done before. It was not in the script.

Gaurang opened his eyes and when he saw his wife, he smiled and sat up. Lata stood up immediately to make room for him. Whether it was the coldness in her eyes or out of habit, Gaurang turned to look at his gun hoister which he usually kept on the table. It was empty.

Lata was doubtful if she would be able to shoot point blank. She realized she could. She also realized that indeed she was looking forward to it.

****

Mahesh knew the man sucking the end of the sugarcane under the neem tree was not just an innocent by-stander. Nargis had told him about all the vantage points from where he will be seen. Uma was an asset. They had spent lakhs on her. If they could not earn at least fifty times from her they were sure to kill her. Either way, it was a death sentence for her. The dead phone felt like a brick in his pocket. He hung his head low and ran inside his house. Fortunately his family members had been visiting the neighbouring village for a cousin's marriage.

Mahesh could hear the moans and cries from the room where he had tied Uma. The sobs broke his heart. There was no doubt that he loved her. But did he love her enough to do as Nargis had asked him to do…. maybe running away was the best thing he could do. Tears of surrender and helplessness drenched his shirt. The image of his lively wife showering him with love clawed at his heart… but he couldn't… just couldn't….

The man under the neem tree was bored. He always got the job of watching people from funny places. The flabbergasted puny man was not even a threat. But orders were orders. The sugarcane was done with and he had nothing better to do. He decided it wouldn't do any harm to rest his legs a little by sitting down. As such it was way past

2 am and there was no activity anywhere, lest in the house. But then, just as he sat down, Mahesh clamored out of the house like a thief, his eyes red shot with unshed tears, his clothes disarrayed, his belongings packed in duffle bags and a large aluminum suitcase. He picked up his luggage and with one last look at the house, he walked away. The man near the tree went to the house and checked the locks. He put his ears to the cracks of the old door. Unmistakable sobs and cries echoed through closed doors... so the mule was there. All was not lost.

****

At least Lata did what she was asked to... child or no child. She was the perfect candidate to be the heir of the empire. Ganga was an odd ball, a genetic deformity, and therefore had to be killed. She had shown great promise, until she fell in love with the fraud Dhayanand and decided to bear his child. She had threatened the boss to expose everything and Tatya knew that she could... but what she hadn't taken into account was that the boss hated loose ends, and rabid greedy dogs. When she was taken to the sea side by her trusted rakhi-brother, she had miscalculated the situation for the first time in her life. She had fought even with 8 months of pregnancy, with all the martial training the boss had given her. She was still alive when they chopped off her fingers and dumped her in the water. Her last thoughts were about her gold toe rings the boss used to reprimand her about... the boss broke the line of thoughts. There was no time to loose. Those who had to go had gone. More will go, but the consignment was due to ship in two days and it would be the last from this location. Soon the place will be grounded. The crime branch will find nothing as usual. But the doctor and the reporter had to be found... well, that was an understatement. The boss knew everything. A small red circle on the map showed exactly where they were, the latitude as well as the longitude. The wait was for them to come out. The doctor had proven way too intelligent for his own life sake, and he had pulled in the reporter... but the boss wanted the girl, Charu, the mule. She was not expendable. The others could die the way they wished to.

****

Mahesh was sitting on the railway station. There was no one following him now. The solitary sleepy station master had grudgingly confirmed that the train to Faridabad was on time. He checked his watch. The approaching light of a slow train alerted him and he stood up at once. As the train came nearer, he frantically looked for coach 2B. The stoppage time for the train for only 2 minutes and it was imperative that he should find that particular coach. It wasn't difficult. The coach was lit and decorated with confetti. The coach was full of drunken relatives of the apparent couple dancing and singing without reserve. Mahesh quickly picked up his luggage and boarded the compartment. He dragged his luggage to the end of the boogie where a single occupant was sitting.

Nargis got up and helped Mahesh bring the aluminum suitcase inside. Then, making sure, that no one was least interested in the mother of the bride, they opened the suitcase. Uma had become so frail that her body fit easily in the box. Mahesh had followed Nargis's instructions and recorded her voice in the phone and asked him to keep it playing on a loop. Mahesh had drugged her with his mother's sleeping pills. Quickly, between them they picked her up, and dressed her in a burkha, made her lie down on the berth and covered her up with a blanket.

If everything went as planned, they would be away from this world of poison by afternoon, the next day. Nargis knew that the boss will quickly trace the missing mule to her. But she had made plans to make herself untouchable. She smiled as she saw Mahesh caress Uma's head lovingly. Love… yes; love… Love is what finally prevails.

＊＊＊＊＊＊＊＊＊＊＊＊

"So you know who the boss is?" Revathi had sat up, her cigarette fallen on the ground.

Charu nodded her head.

"No one knows. I… I sort of volunteered to be a mule. I knew something about the boss. Often Kasturi would blabber about the boss in one of her frenzies. I thought, if I could get inside the ring, I could avenge her death. During one such training when we were taught how to hide the cocaine in our body, I saw her. …Ganga. Initially I thought she was one of the mules. But then she …she …made her men hold the girls while she made them swallow the pills and push the pellets in their insides. She had so much liberty. She would wear gold toe rings… the boss abhorred it... said it was an insult to Laxman, but Ganga would laugh. I tried peeking at the boss but it was always a voice on the phone, or a note left in a hurry. Whenever the henchmen used to tell her something she would laugh. She would go to the Lord and stay there. And then, one day, there was a fight. Ganga wouldn't do what she was asked to… said she loved the Lord. And then we never saw her. Until…..”

Revathi was pacing around. Mohini could not be the big player. The boss had so much power and invisibility that it had to be someone right in front of them. Her thoughts returned to the film.

“Charu, where are the other 23 girls?”

“We were supposed to assemble in the Lord's house; even those who were staying in the other house.”

Sagar, who had been stroking the fire, looked up suddenly.

“The other house?”

“Yes… the other house. The factory.”

Sagar was quiet for some time. The crackling of the twigs getting engulfed in the fire was the only sound for some time before Sagar asked Revathi a very strange question.

“Revathi, that day, when I called you in your office, who else was there? I mean except Mohini?”

“Mohini? Mohini? I don't even know who this Mohini is. I was all alone. The staff had left for the lunch break. I had stayed back because the Editor wanted the last and final draft of the story to be printed in the next edition."

"The editor? Who is he?"

Revathi let out a shrill laugh and lit another cigarette.

"Why do you men always assume that because the term editor is a common noun, it has to be a man? My editor is a woman and also the owner of the newspaper. It is only because of her that the drug circulation had been tamed in our village."

"You mean, she was there when you took the call?"

"Yes… Keva Bai" faltered Revathi, remembering something about Sagar blabbering about a click.

"Since how long has Keva Bai owned the newspaper?"

"Since her family was killed on the bridge…."

"And the film your father had was 'lost'?"

"Since the film was lost…"

CHAPTER THIRTY ONE

Keva Bai

Tatya might look like the extra in a cheap Hindi flick with his rotund belly and walrus moustache; but under all that were years of experience. The spattered brains of his boss on the wall, and the strange squint distorting his features, indicated that he had been shot point blank. The service pistol in his right hand and everything else, including the stunned shell shocked wife fitted the frame so well that Tatya could not swallow it.

For one, he knew that his boss was not a good man, and although a seedling of conscience was growing within him, his greed was much bigger. Also, Tatya had seen him carry the stash from the Lord's house, and it had been missing. He had looked everywhere. He knew that it wasn't his responsibility, and he will never be questioned, but yet… he wanted to know where the cocaine had disappeared.

His first guess was that the drug mafia had caught up with PI Gaurang and done off with him. He was about to leave it at that… the wife, Lata, was like a sister to him. Her hollowed eyes and tender health condition concerned him. He went up to her and laid a kind hand on her shoulder. That is when he noticed her feet caked in mud.

Instinctively his eyes were drawn to the garden. A patch of newly upturned land was squarely marked out. Lata followed Tatya's eyes. Tatya was breathing heavily… he shouted for a shovel, and lifted his hands from her shoulder.

"Dada, I have to tell you something…"

"Lata, how could you?"

"I had no choice…."

"No choice? He had changed. And what were you planning with the stash?"

Lata was silent and stoic; she neither moved nor spoke. Tatya took the shovel and started to dig vigorously, the soft soil yielding easily. It seemed whatever had been buried had been buried in a shallow grave.

"Dada, I don't understand what you are saying."

Lata was dry heaving now, finding it difficult to speak. Tatya's shovel stopped about 3 feet inside the ground when he picked up something folded in a plastic bag.

"Dada, they kicked me 6 times, after shooting him. After an hour my child aborted. I did not know what to do… and I knew that the police would be interested in Gaurang's murder more than me… so I wrapped him, and buried him deep… there are dogs here you see.…"

Lata could not finish her sentence, and Tatya almost throwing down the bloody bag with the unborn fetus. He was ashamed of what he had just done. He comforted Lata and reburied the mortal remains. Then he left with his squad, the ambulance packing up the body of the dead PI. Lata locked the bedroom and returned to her garden where she had submerged the stash in the well. Her child felt safe in her belly; she was amused as how similar fetuses of humans and animals look at 3-4 months. She pulled out the bundle wrapped in plastic and waited for the next call. It was time for her next life.

＊＊＊＊＊＊＊＊＊＊＊＊

"I know someone who can get the film developed." Charu had suddenly remembered her tourist photographer.

A satellite phone was used to call a very surprised and reluctant photographer to develop the ancient reels of questionable quality. Although, Sagar had a very good idea of what they would find in the photographs, he couldn't understand the reason or the intension behind whatever the woman was doing. The trio were still trying to add up the facts which concluded that the benign, philanthropic woman fighting against the drug syndicate was likely the syndicate herself. She had to be the boss. She had been the reason behind the murder of hundreds of innocent young men and women… apparently she had also killed her own family.

****

How was she going to have things done? The new girls were inapt. The Lord had to die now?. The inspector had to steal at no better time? Three of the 24 girls were gone; one was dead. One had escaped somehow, and Charu seemed to be stuck at some point in the jungle, neither moving, nor running. Mohini was not in the hospital, but her men had seen the nurse and that Ratan carry an unusually huge bag and fling it in the incinerator. The ship was to move the next night. The girls were safe… but something was tugging at her bosom.

Keva Bai was sitting in front of the five photographs on the wall highlighted by the yellow spot lights….it had all started with her. Bile rose in her chest as she looked at the beautiful laughing girl with dark long hair. Today, the factory was apparently empty. But she knew that hidden in the recesses were twenty odd women of ages ranging from 16-30 who had no choice but to stuff themselves with the pellets and go where they are sent off to. The place sobbed silently of their helplessness… or was the heaves coming from Keva Bai? Was the boss finally grieving her sons?

Keva had been a child bride when she came to the Bapat family at the age of 13. Her husband Laxman Rao Bapat was fifteen years her senior, and therefore she had no excuse but to bear three children in quick successions. Ganga was the eldest and was followed by the twins. Their family business was that of edible oil and was a flourishing one.

Rich as they were, Laxman Rao did not believe in giving his wife any money. The young woman, tempted by the latest fashions, would try and find ways to get her hands on the newest things. That is when someone handed her a small white packet and asked her to send it to an address. The simple job earned her enough money for a pair of new earrings. Feisty and courageous as she was, her job descriptions became more and more daring and treacherous. Her husband who was already wed to his family business neither cared nor worried. Keva was happy. She could bring up her children as she wanted to.

The twins were the apple of her eyes. But in Ganga she saw her own unruly behavior; her disregard of rules and boundaries. As the children grew, so did Keva's power as the brain and heart of the very live drug devil thriving on the poverty and simplicity of the people. Keva chose the men and women to carry the drugs, on her own. Then she started taking in girls like Mohini who had no soul. She also trained both men and women to kill and be lethal with weapons, because in her business the possibility of death was always a close companion occupying the nearby seat.

Soon she had expanded her business overseas and it was worth in hundreds of crores. She mollified her mind and occasionally questioning soul by doing civil work for the village. She had helped the fishing industry and employed the women but everything was just her own way of getting her things done. Everything would have been fine. She had shipped the boys to London to keep them out of it all. Her in-laws had died, none the wiser. And her husband and his brother, although had supposedly got a whiff of her doings could do nothing more than turn up their nose in disdain. Because even they could not deny that she had increased their worth by many folds.

Then Ganga had to come back from America, all grown up and beautiful… in a week she had befriended Mohini in the most infamous way, and gleaned all she wanted to know. One fine day, she joined the army of women and men training to be assassins. Keva did not want any of her children to be involved in the syndicate; but Ganga had just laughed, and later proved to be the most ruthless assassin Keva had ever trained. On several failed deals she had nonchalantly pulled out her Berretta and her serrated knives to settle the deals. Keva saw the future in her hands until she met the fraudster Dhayanand and fell in love with him. Keva had miscalculated that a woman who could hate and kill with such impasse could love with the same insane abstruse passion. Helplessly, Keva saw as Ganga made herself his mistress.

She had sent several newspaper cuttings to Dhayanand to frighten him; clearly stating that she knew all about him murdering his family. For years he had arranged and loaded mules with efficacy. But Keva was ready to sacrifice him if that meant saving her daughter. She had sent her best to finish him. The same day, Ganga had come to her mother while she was having her tea, dressed in a red saree, her toes clad in gold rings, she sat in the chair opposite, and put a hand on that of her mother. Keva was relieved… her daughter was back. Her smile turned into a scream as Ganga placed a severed head on the table just beside the cup of tea. The Henchman's face was contoured in a frozen scream.

"Bhima and Keshav are coming in a week's time." She had said in a matter of fact kind of way. But the threat was very real. Keva knew that Ganga knew that the boys were her Achilles heel. While the boys were around, she could do nothing.

And then the boys had landed, fresh, innocent, untouched, and in awe of their mother. Keva sunk deeper into the arm chair. Why? Why did they have to come? Tears welled up in her eyes and rolled down her cheeks: Her innocent boys. The fateful day swam behind her closed eyes as if it was just yesterday…

It had been after a fiasco by Mohini when she had tried to rope in a local boy called Ratan. But unknown to her, Ratan was a very close friend of her sons and couldn't have chosen a worse time to try and recruit him. What Keva did not know as at then was that Mohini had been directed towards Ratan by Ganga. It had been Ganga's plan to instigate Mohini to go after him so that the boys would later question their mother. Her aim was to get rid of the outsider Mohini and at the same time take care of the insider… her mother. She knew that finding the culprit as one of their mother's close employees would put the seed of doubt in the boys' head and then it would be just a matter of exposing her in the newspapers, and bringing her empire crashing down. She had already collaborated with Dhayanand and seduced the poor thing into doing as he was told.

The leading reporter started getting abnormal number of tips regarding next meetings. Consignments and the exact amount of goods changing hands found its way in the reporter's diary. But he was forbidden by the benefactor to act upon the knowledge as yet… not yet, she had said on the phone. It had been a Saturday when Ganga came to her mother's office and shut the door behind her. Keva Bai was taken aback and a little defensive… as she had become a little afraid of her recently. But she looked genuinely concerned and the mother's heart softened. Seating herself, Ganga took out an envelope from her purse. She leaned forward, worry etched on her beautiful face.

"Ma, I got this yesterday. It was left on the table."

Keva tore open the envelope. There were ten coloured photographs of Ganga and Dhayanand in compromising positions. Ganga burst into tears. Keva stood up and hugged her daughter. Who so ever had done it had done the family a favor. Of course he would want money but at least Keva would get back her daughter.

"What is he asking for?"

"He says that the photographs will be in the evening newspaper… unless… unless I pay him"

"You speak as if you know him dear. Who is he?"

"Reporter Jayendra."

The tightening of the grip on her shoulder told Ganga that the journalist was not good news. It also alerted her a little. The web she had been spinning slowly and steadily seemed to be unraveling from another end; yet Ganga decided to continue with her part. In her focus, she had forgotten that the men in the Bapat family valued honor more than life. Neither had she anticipated the sudden appearance of her brothers in the office.

The photographs lying sprawled on the table in an obscene display were enough to make the brothers mad with rage. Ganga who had posed for the pictures was unsure how to cool off the unpredicted uproar of her siblings. She loved her brothers; not because of their goodness, but because they posed no threat to her direct claim over the kingdom.

Soon the father and uncle were involved, and although the phototo was not shown, the journalist's name was discussed. Ganga, her head hung low and her mind in a whirl, was trying to turn the events her way. She was quickly losing the empathy she had gained, and was quickly being toed around… and that she could not tolerate. It was time to take out the ace. With eyes swimming with tears she looked at her mother.

"I… I did not want to bring it up Ma. But there was one more envelope."

Keva was no fool. The smile forming at the corners of her daughter's lips were not missed. She knew just what was coming up. She watched as Ganga fished out the other packet. Everyone was looking at her, but Keva was looking at her sons with trepidation. She walked a couple of steps back as if subconsciously trying to distance herself from their pain at the revelation the photographs were going to cause. She turned towards the window, her eyes blurred with the world moving at a crazy speed in front of her eyes. There was silence and just the rustling of paper as the photographs changed hands.

"Ma, who are all these people? I never knew that you knew so many of them…" Bhīma's innocence was heart wrenching.

"They are drug mafias from different countries, son…" Laxman Rao had no qualms at exposing his lowly wife anymore. Like lightening Keva's brother-in-law was upon her plummeting her with punches and blows. Bhima and Keshav, in spite of everything could not bear to see their mother being assaulted and humiliated and came to her aide. It was yet a news way too big for them to completely comprehend and understand that the drug addiction which their family had apparently been fighting and standing up for was exactly the thing which was paying for their education.

The brothers wrestled their uncle and easily overpowered him. Keva looked at her boys and their broken trust killed her soul. Then she looked at Ganga… Ganga, her first born… her splitting image… someone who was just as she was, and her mouth filled with bile. Keva knew that she had already lost her sons… but she would end the story with Ganga. She would pay the price of taking a mother's children away from her.

"Ma, if this is true… I know someone must have misled you. Let us all go to the police and surrender. Ma… Ma?" Keshav was shaking Keva by her arm. Surrender? If she did that, she knew that there were people above her who would not blink an eye to wipe out her whole family. How could she explain to her sons that she could not turn back? And what had Ganga done in her hunger for power and narcissism? Didn't she realize the death sentence she had just written for her brothers and her father and uncle?

"Bhima, Keshav, sons, please I beg of you. Please go back to London and don't come back again… I cannot surrender. I am sorry…."

The boys moved away, their hands clasped to their faces as the truth dawned upon them completely. After what seemed like an eternity, Bhima spoke up.

"Ma, you will surrender. Or else either way, we are going to the police. If they don't listen, we will go to Crime Branch. I don't care why you can't surrender, but we will stop it…."

A knock on the door shook everyone out of their shock. The least expected visitor was standing on the doorway, his camera hung on his neck and a smug smile on his face. As a rule, Keva never kept any of her henchmen in her residence. Their absence suddenly made her feel vulnerable. How the journalist had got the whiff of the family drama was anyone's guess. But Keva knew that it had to be orchestrated by Ganga in some way.

"I see the good versus the bad part is going on! Did you like my photographs Keva Bai?" Journalist Jayendra was irritating and cocky.

"What do you want? We are going to the crime branch. There is nothing for you to scavenge here. And as far as my sister's photos are concerned, you can take the money and get lost."

"What are you talking about? What sister's photos? Anyways, you think your mother the great Keva Bai will surrender and give away her empire?" The uproarious laugh was sarcastic. The journalist knew that a surrender would not even shake the branches of the deep rooted vice which had gripped his village. He also knew that Keva Bai would rather kill than stop her shipments… he had other plans. He had taken enough evidence to convict the seven major drug junctions in the world. With collaborations from other major newspapers, he was planning on a documentary and a breaking-news.

"Ok, I will surrender."

Ganga stood up her grin, out of place and averse to the situation. Bhima and Keshav came and hugged their mother. Laxman Bapat grunted and walked away accompanied with his brother. Only Jayendra looked at the woman straight in the eye. He had seen the eyes through the safety of his camera lens a million times. But today, the soullessness in the eyes scared the otherwise plucky journalist. He looked on as she hugged her boys close to her heart and stared straight ahead neither blinking nor shedding a tear. Something had broken in Keva. She had chosen her path, and she had closed her heart for what was coming, because she knew that if she didn't, then she would not be able to survive it.

The plan was to send the journalist with all the evidence with Laxman Rao and his brother in the car which had been tampered with.

Keva was sure that she would be successful in dissuading her sons from going. She spent the whole night pleading with them to go back to London. When they finally agreed, Keva was happy and relieved. But then in the morning the boys were already dressed up and ready to go. They had decided to spare their mother the embarrassment and face the crime branch instead of her. Keva held them back… no don't go in the car… how could she tell them? The brakes had been disabled? She ran behind them… but it was too late.

"No… no…. no… don't go!"

The empty factory echoed with the screams of a mother who had pushed her innocent sons to death. The weight of their demise was heavier than all the other things she had done over the decades. Her soul split into multiple fragments had lost the capability to mend and therefore she had decided that after this shipment, she would hand over the ropes to Lata. In the absence of Mohini and Nargis, she had asked Lata to take over.

When the torrent of tears had settled, Keva Bai turned her thoughts to more important things. She was short of three mules and with the stash Lata had brought back, she needed them soon. There was no time for new passports, and therefore the old ones had to be used. Someone like Phooli, Uma and Charu were needed… but Charu was not dead… Lata needed to be told. For a moment Keva Bai's eyes darted towards the photograph of a younger Ganga and relief washed over her. Vengeance was sweet; even if that meant watching one's own daughter die.

CHAPTER THIRTY TWO

The Evidence

The photographer had already packed and parceled off his family and personal belongings to Puri. He knew that once the photographs he was holding saw the daylight, he and his family would be dead. Several times it had crossed his mind that he was being foolish by agreeing to do something so senselessly dangerous for someone who did not even matter to him. But the lure of money and the basic instinct of watching gibberish plastic metamorph into colorful stories gave him enough momentum to finish developing the decade old reel.

He did not waste time going through all of them and bundled them in a newspaper. The doctor had volunteered to collect them from him and pass on the said fees. He saw the doctor shivering in the cold from the crack of the door... it felt like years before when he had saved this particular man's life. The photographer mellowed down a bit at the memory, and justified that finally he was doing something on the side of truth. He opened the door and handed the waiting doctor the photos. The doctor held out two thick silver anklets which the photographer accepted and shut the door quickly. As far as he was concerned, the deal was done.

The doctor felt a bit sad at having to hand over the anklets Charu had volunteered as payment as none of the trio had any money. He walked on the deserted street feeling the weight of the photographs in his pocket. At the corner of the road, a street light was miraculously working and was in very good condition. Sagar stood under the lamp post and ran a hand over his beard. Finally, he sat down and took out the photographs and went through all of them. It was almost midnight before he stood up on rickety legs and somehow managed to walk to the safe house.

Charu surprisingly welcomed him with a resounding slap, while Revathi looked on with a fresh cigarette butt littering the floor.

"Where were you all these while?" Charu was hysterical. Her face was hot with tears. Her feet and legs were scratched because she had tried trailing Sagar in the dark.

Sagar blinked twice. So naked was her love for him that nothing else mattered. He ran to her and took her in his arms; as she wept with reckless abandon. Only when Sagar thought that he could manage to shift his head did he tilt her towards himself, and kissed her. Charu, her dreams and reality clashing and merging into one like the waves of the sea, realized that she had received all she wanted… now even death was welcome. Now, she could tell Sagar what was on her mind….

Revathi was relieved that Charu had stopped screaming, Sagar had finally confirmed his love, and that the photos were ready. It's time again for the hacking cough.

"I think you should stop smoking." Charu was back at being cheerful and acid tongued.

"Doc, where are the photos? I presume you have seen them all. We could have done it here. You jeopardized your life unnecessarily."

"The shipment is tomorrow. I don't think Keva Bai will do anything drastic today… and here are all the evidences we need to incriminate her as well as the connected syndicates. And I need to go to the clinic."

Both the women left whatever they were doing and looked at him.

"Why?" they asked in union.

"I must see someone. Someone who must have known everything from the start."

****

The knock on the door could not be good news. It was four in the morning and the photographer was not expecting anyone; not even the milkman. His small suitcase was already locked and tied up in a bed-sheet with the anklets inside them. The train tickets in his pockets. He decided to ignore the person who-so-ever it was. For a moment he thought the doctor had come back. The knock came back again. Somebody called out in a very sweet and innocent voice. A woman: what was a woman doing at his door-steps? And did she just say Charu's name?

"Charu? Charu, child? Vaini is here child!" The knock became a little more urgent. The photographer could sense the urgency and concern in the woman's voice. But for all he knew, Charu did not have any living relative…. Suddenly the voice became heavier as if the woman was going to cry.

"Charu, will you not forgive your unfortunate sister? Please child… look, I am pregnant, and I am standing in the cold…."That was all the photographer needed to hear. He rose and opened the door. A petite and thin woman in nothing more than a saree looked blankly at him. She was neither crying, nor smiling.

"Where is she?" The coldness in her tone told the photographer that he had made a very grave mistake by opening the door.

"Who?" The aghast photographer faltered. The woman pushed past him in his one room house and looked around. There was no place a full grown woman could hide. But the tracker had shown this particular house… unless.

"Where are the anklets?"

"What anklets?" He was not going to let some wuss steal from him. And as such, she was only about half his size and he could just push her out.

Lata came close to the photographer, her eyes slightly enlarged like that of a doe's.

"Bhau, please tell me where the anklets are; or keep them; but tell me, where is Charu… please?"

There was such a plea in her voice that the photographer's opinion regarding her kept oscillating. Now she seemed so innocent, so caring… how would it hurt to tell her where Charu was?

"She is in a van under the bridge…."

"Bhau, you are like God to me! How can I thank you?" Lata stepped four steps back and before the photographer could think of ways she could repay him, the bullet went through his head.

More than once Lata had seen him glancing at the pathetic suitcase. Lata knew that the anklet would be there. She galumphed on the cheap contraption and the contents spilled out. The anklets were hidden at the bottom. Lata picked them up and turned off the tracker. Then without looking at anything else she simply walked out of the house, her last thoughts being that the woman of the house was a lousy housekeeper.

CHAPTER THIRTY-THREE

Confessions

"When you decided to go to the clinic, did you counsel with me?"

"That is preposterous. Going to the clinic is not same as stuffing drugs in my body, and going to a God forbidden country, knowing that either way you will die. No Charu, you are not going…"

Charu had disclosed to Sagar that she had to go because she could not stay hidden all her life. She knew that although Sagar loved her, there was no future with them together. She was so close to getting to her sister's killers. She wanted to get them or die doing so.

"Ok, if you want to go, at least wait till I come back from the clinic… you can do that?" Charu did not look at him. She just stood and shook her head. Sagar and Revathi had managed to get hold of a vehicle going towards the city. They had to get out and risk everything to get food and money. Had they turned and looked back, they would have seen a woman covered in a red shawl making her way on foot on the dirt road towards the bridge.

For Charu, the mere thought that she may never be seeing Sagar again dissolved her into uncontrollable sobs. She remembered how he had kissed her. She would carry the feeling and the warmth of his body like a talisman. Encouraged by her own words, Charu quickened her pace. She clamoured over the debris and silt and reached the broken bridge. She knew that the Lord's house would be a useless endeavor.

They had already been informed about the dead and the raid. Charu knew where she had to go. The factory was at the other end of the backwater and she needed a dingy to take her there.

****

Ratan and nurse were bound in an inevitable bond which binds people who had cheated death. After they had seen the incinerator truck ramble away, they had gone to the nurse's house because Ratan had no place to go, his own house still a sad and dangerous place. The nurse had seen most of the youngsters grow up into men, and having had no children of her own, she would be especially heartbroken whenever anyone of them was taken away by the evil of drugs.

She still remembered the day Ratan was picked up by Bhima and Keshav and they had refused to take him to the clinic. She also remembered the day Mohini, then younger had recruited him. And then… and then… the boys had died.

Ratan was looking around her small garden, especially interested in the marigolds and bougainvillea. She invited him inside. She realized that neither had eaten anything. Ratan had been kind to her. Had it not been for him, she would have been dead. The same could be said for him though.

The nurse prepared a simple meal of rice and potatoes and served it in two plates. After they had finished, she waited till Ratan was calm enough to hear what she had to tell him. She thought that she owed the good man that much… maybe, maybe some of her own sins would reduce? Who was she kidding? If Keva Bai was the life of the drug demon, hadn't she been the one to have fed the demon?

****

Dr. Sagar must have looked really bad by the expression of the ward boy. Only later did it occur to him that the gaping mouth and terrified eyes were probably because of the fact that Sagar had been presumed dead. The total absence of patients hurt him. But he was looking for something else.

He went to his office, where the red tape spelling his name had been replaced by some other name. Expecting to find someone else in the office, he knocked before he entered. His office was in shambles. Someone had run through his things looking for something. It did not matter anymore. What he needed was as such not there. He called out to the ward boy who was already standing near the door, his mouth closed and some of his composure back.

"Where is the staff register?"

"We… we… don't have it any more. The last doctor destroyed everything."

Dr. Sagar ran his hands through his hair. That day amongst the many people in the photographs, he had seen a very familiar face. She was always in the background, withdrawn, as if sorry to be there… but never-the-less there. She was younger, but her identity was undeniable.

"Raju, where is nurse?"

"She went home for lunch, sir."

"Raju, what is our nurse's name?"

Raju looked perplexed as he heard the doctor asking this apparently irrelevant question.

"Shanti Bapat, sir… her name is Shanti Bapat."

****

Ratan listened with deepening anger as Shanti Bapat revealed how Keva Bai had created the whole empire and appointed people to do the dirty work, while she kept up the pristine image of the ideal woman and philanthropist. She told him how she was the one responsible for deaths of many including her Phooli. Also, she told him that the rumor that she had killed her own sons was true.

The anger which had sort of pacified with the death of Mohini surged up so fast that he could not control the blinding pain behind his eyes. Tears of frustration and anger burst forth. He had revered the woman… but all the time she had been orchestrating the whole circus. Phooli… his innocent Phooli; how many more had she swallowed: his innocent friends Bhima and Keshav, her own children? If there was someone who deserved to die, it was her.

****

"How do you know all this?"

"Because she is Shanti Bapat… wife of Bapat, sister-in-law to Keva Bai, and aunt to your friends."

The doctor had expected surprise from his longtime associate. Instead, there was only guilt and sorrow.

"Yes, she was my sister-in-law. But I was always in the shadow. I never wanted to be a part of this syndicate. I never touched the money. Rather I tried to find out all the youngsters she had been trying to recruit and treat them… but then… she killed them. She killed them all… her own blood and flesh. Not once but twice. What do you think Dr. Sagar; had I any chance in front of her? Yes, but I did not stand up for myself and let things happen… when each child I had seen grow up died, a part of me died with them… and yes Dr. Sagar, I knew the woman they found in the red saree and gold toe rings was Ganga, Keva's first born. I had pleaded with her to let her go… at least to let the child be born. But she insisted. She wanted to take her child away from her just as years back she had staged the circumstance which caused her sons' death."

The confession seemed to have aged the nurse by several years. The bandage under her chin had slipped off, soaked with tears. Ratan came near her and sat down. Then he hugged the old woman.

"You may have been a dumb witness to evil, but your kindness and courage has saved so many, including me. Had you not hidden me,

I would have been dead meat. Shanti, you are more than any hapless aid. You are the mother I never had…." The old nurse dissolved into tears. It was as if she had been granted salvation. The doctor was also nodding his head in silent but strong agreement. It was time.

****

Revathi had seen the oddly familiar woman ransacking through their van. That there was no sign of Charu and Revathi was relieving and worrying in equal measures. It was certain by the ominous looking gun hanging from her waist that the woman had murder on her mind and was really unhappy that she had found the place empty. At the same time Revathi was concerned about Charu. Was it possible that the stupid child had finally done what she had been talking about? Revathi dropped the packets of food and change of clothes she had brought along with her silently to the ground, making sure not to make any sound what-so-ever. Then she retraced her steps… very slowly. She had no intensions of dying. Not yet. Not until she had the news out for the public. She looked at her watch. Twenty four hours to go… was she late already?

CHAPTER THIRTY-FOUR

Time for Business

The four winged factory was just the façade… the top skin. Underneath was a gory city of helplessness, drug addiction, and greed. Everyday died there and there was the favorite game, called 'Didis', the elders who had survived being mules, and because of their resilience and greed to be a part of something their ordinary lives back in the village could not provide, had been retained in the organization specially for days like today.

The underground city was nothing more than a long dormitory-like tunnel lit by artificial light to simulate the sun. Four toilets lined the opposite walls, not for convenience and sanitation, but for cleaning out the bowels of the mules with enemas before they would be 'adorned'. This time all the mules were women. There was an eerie silence in the dungeon like room as the Didis worked on filling up condoms with carefully counted pellets. Each condom could hold 30-35 pellets. The ends were tied.

Occasionally some lewd joke about the size of the condom would make the Didis roll on the ground with laughter. Otherwise, there was hardly any sound from the mules that had been already cleaned and placed with plates of soft fruits like chickoos and bananas embedded with the drug so that it made it easier for them to swallow them. After thre days of being kept away from any kind of food, even poison was acceptable to them.

Lata had hardly been into the undergrounds. She was an assassin and found this kind of work below her. But when she had called the boss to tell her about her inability to find Charu, she had been surprised to know that the girl had returned to the factory on her own account. The edge in the softness in the boss' voice as she instructed Lata that she was needed in the underground to load the mules was unmistakable. The unforgiving woman had never taken a no for an answer…. Lata had to go. And so, here she was, amidst the filthy, frail, almost dying, and some, surprisingly well kept women of all ages, sitting in a line, their knees drawn to their chests, their lower half naked as instructed to them.

She wanted to see Charu; for no other reasons other than the fact that she wanted to see the person who had enchanted her glorious, valiant, and now sadly demised, husband. She was pointed to an extraordinarily beautiful and young girl who sat with her legs apart, her eyes open and looking around, unlike the others who had shut off their eyes in an effort to forget all of it like a dream. Lata saw the absence of fear in those large eyes, and knew at once that she was bad news.

"Didi, did you start the loading yet? There are twenty bitches. They will take a lot of time. Plus the clothing and the make up to make them look like aristocrats…. Shall we start? I will start with this one." But Charu was already on her feet. She had done it severally and knew exactly what was needed to be done. She collected the required amount of pellets and expertly inserted them all in her cavities.

"Maybe some more… Charu?" With that Lata progressed to carry the duck billed contraption lying on the table.

"Lata Vaini, she has had enough…" The worker stopped midway. Lata was staring at her with cold eyes. The worker bent her head and started unrolling condoms to fill them up with pellets. When she had turned back, Charu had already slipped into another portion of the ant hill.

The elder women were easier to load; most of them could do it themselves. What really challenged the workers were the younger unwed girls. On many occasions, Mohini had been instructed to refrain from using such girls. But the crazy woman just wanted her list of recruits to grow bigger and better.

A scream tore the silence of the underground, followed by piteous cries of mercy. Someone was asking to be left alone and allowed to go home. Lata loitered lazily in the direction of the commotion. There was always someone who would create unnecessary drama. This time, it was a 15 year old with her legs high up in straps as if she was getting ready for a gynecological examination. Two women were buried elbow deep into her anus and vagina. Blood was dripping slowly on the floor. None of the women wore gloves.

"What's wrong?" the women moved aside. Lata came to survey the situation. As always, a 15 year old was too small for the whole load.

"Where is the duck?"

The duck was the name of the colposcope they used to open the vagina wide to access. The women looked at each other. It was a cruel metal instrument which was only reserved for women who had given birth at least once. But they quietly handed her the duck, called so because of its duck bill like opening.

Lata, humming something like a lullaby inserted the duck bill scope inside the girl: the contraption four times bigger than her apertures. The lullaby did not stop even after the screams continued. The women standing there could see the edges of the girl's vagina beginning to tear.

"Lata Vaini, this really hurts… will keep the girl scarred for life."

"Is that so?" Lata inserted the scope deeper as the perineum tore wider. The million times Gaurang had raped her brought an involuntary tear in her eye… the helplessness, the pain… she knew it all. She knew exactly what the girl was feeling. The lullaby had stopped. She reproached herself for her temporary weakness. The fast ticking in her belly seemed as if her child was also reprimanding her… she started to sing again. The scope went further in till the pink cervix was seen. She asked for the stash and filled up the girl who was now unconscious with pain and fatigue.

"Stitch her up. Or else she will purge as soon as she squats. And she will not be of any use later. Throw her…."

The child kicked again. Lata smiled. This was one notorious child she was going to have…

****

When Nargis crossed the smartly dressed woman in white, she could sense that both had tensed up. Nargis had a fairly good idea that the woman passing by was actually 'the boss'. Keva Bai recognized Nargis at once and was happy and relieved to see her here but a direct question might give her away. Both acknowledged the other with a civil nod but there was palpable tension. Nargis wondered who was more afraid of whom… considering the facts, she thought that if Allah willed things to happen her way, it would be she who would be having the last laugh of the day.

Nargis walked inside the factory, and she knew that Keva Bai would find some excuse or the other to follow her. After all, the new girl Uma had been entrusted to her and now she was missing. Nargis knew that the tracker they had placed on her had been dislodged while she was struggling on the ropes Mahesh had used to tie her…. Uma and Mahesh… Nargis's eyes filled up at their thought. God bless them wherever they were. Sure enough she heard footsteps approaching her.

CHAPTER THIRTY-FIVE

End to Lawlessness

The supervisor was having the sterling moment of her life. She was surprised and extremely pleased to see the old worker walk inside the room. For a moment all work stopped as all eyes were upon her. The supervisor, her teeth drawn in a sardonic grin ran to the only person she thought was in command, Lata, to tell her all about the elusive Nargis who was probably responsible for the disappearance of Uma, one of the mules. Lata was scrutinizing Nargis from head to toe. Like a predator about to pounce on her quarry, she approached the quivering woman.

"Well, well, well… the celebrated prodigal worker returns. But we don't need workers, we need mules… and I think she will do."

"I… I cannot tolerate any amount of the drug… the boss knows. Ganga knew. I want to talk to Keva madam for a moment before I come back to my work."

A sudden shift… a sudden shuffle behind the curtains told Nargis that her targeted audience was right where she wanted her to be. Nargis walked towards the main office, the supervisor, and Lata, unsure what they should be doing next. By the time Nargis had reached the office, Lata was already there.

But madam, I tell you, she is the one… or else how do we explain finding the company phone in her house with the recordings of the woman's cries? The track was found beside the bed… there were people who had seen her talking to her in the bus… madam; I tell you, let's tear her legs apart and…."

"Lata, leave her to me. Nargis doesn't work for you. She is an old friend, and I shall deal with her. Please leave us alone."

Lata fumed. Rebuked, she had learnt to be silent thanks to her late husband. But also, thanks to him again, she had learnt how to reply to rebuke at the right time and place.

****

"I know you did it."

"I know that you are the boss, Keva Bai."

Keva Bai was silent for a long time. Nargis had been one of her first recruits; her first and last mistake. She had been a loose cannon ball. Only after her family had been threatened did she agree to settle down working in the factory as one of the workers; and of them all, her association with Keva Bai was the longest.

"Then you also know that the mules cost a lot of money. Once their passports are made, it becomes virtually impossible to replace them. Do you know…?"

"I did not come here to talk about Uma, Keva Bai. I came to talk about you."

"Me? What about me?"

"I want to save your life."

Keva Bai wanted to laugh out loud. Who could touch her? She was the empress… the boss. And this lowly woman in torn clothes was trying to save her life?

Nargis took the smirk on her face as disbelief. She had already started to fidget on her chair, considering the meeting to be over. Nargis reached inside her purse and pulled out stacks of photographs. Keva just had to take one look at them to know that the graveyard of a past hidden had been unearthed… how was that possible. She had made sure that then photographs were destroyed… unless Ganga…. Ganga must have made a copy.

"What do you want?"

"I want total immunity for each and every member of my family as well as Uma and her husband. "

"And how do you propose to save me?"

Nargis fished out a battered green Bangladeshi passport from her bag. "Keva Bai, do you have a pair of spectacles? Because… I can't see without them…."

✳✳✳✳✳✳✳✳✳✳✳✳✳

The new inspector, who had joined after PI Gaurang, was fresh as a daisy. Moreover, it was his first posting. What years of experience he lacked, his pluck and love of adventure made up for him adequately. Within a short span of taking charge of the office, the new PI Madhavan had taken care of all small pesky crimes. But his eyes were on the wide spread web of the drug mafia which had brought the silent non-descript village on the world map. To find out its roots and chop off the source had become the sole motto of the young inspector. The older team headed by seasoned and have-seen-it-all officers like Tatya had also accepted the veritability of the feisty inspector.

The unlikely trio of a villager, a nurse, and an extremely shaggy doctor considered dead, sitting in the police station, relating the most unusual tale, was increasing the trepidation of the ending for the inspector who was looking forward to it as a child does to a video game. On every discreet mention of the police being involved, PI Madhavan would look at the increasingly uncomfortable and sweaty Tatya who would reply with a cough that would either mean a yes or no, according to the circumstances. Each one's story was supported by the other.

Aliases were verified, and the doctor had had the presence of mind to get all the real autopsy reports.

"But there is one problem. All these five or six odd women… they were unclaimed. They don't even have a name. That does not mean we don't have a case. Anonymous or named, a murder is a murder." The inspector looked at his spectators for the effect of his speech. While Tatya, standing out of his perimeter of vision was rolling his eyes, the three civilians were nodding in agreement. But something seemed to be bothering the nurse. Shanti Bapat could not shake off the feeling. It was something the inspector had said; something about 'all' the bodies being anonymous.

CHAPTER THIRTY-SIX

The Army of convenience

The woman was being scrutinized like cattle for sale. The supervisor had found her loitering near the factory and concluded that her features matched that of the dead girl Phooli and could easily pass as her. She was healthy and clueless about what was going on. There was no time for the long process of induction and preparation. She took the girl directly to the underground room and left her with Lata. Nargis was nowhere to be seen. Just as the girl was supposed to be subject to the same treatment as others, Lata's phone rang.

A quiet, calm voice spoke in its characteristic baritone, asking Lata to start boarding all the mules to the orange dingy anchored at bay. Lata was confused. There was no mistaking the fact that it was the boss, but why was she calling her on a phone now that everyone knew her identity. Never-the-less, she shrugged her shoulders and shouted the order to all the workers. The new girl was forgotten in the following chaos; and she quickly searched the heard of black heads and found the curly head she was interested in.

When Charu saw the black tan Revathi had applied on her face, she laughed out loud. Then she calmed down; just too glad to have a friend with her in such a difficult time. Quickly Revathi whispered what was going to happen next in her ear.

****

Nurse Shanti Bapat wiped her perspiration as she ended the call. Trying to talk emotionlessly and coldly like her sister-in-law had been taxing. She was surprised that the right hand of the boss had accepted the call. As soon as the call was done, PI Madhavan put his force into action.

Already several teams in ordinary civilian clothes were in strategic locations. He stared at his watch; and calculated that they had exactly 45 minutes to intercept the dingy and catch them in the act. That is if the backwaters were high. Or else things would be different. They would cancel the plan and the consignment would go earlier from a different port with the mules being transported by land.

Keva Bai's army was impressive and armed with the latest armaments. The age old wooden handled service pistols of the police force would have no chance against them, Madhavan knew. His strategy was to infiltrate at two levels. First, he had collaborated with the feisty journalist Revathi to get herself into the herd of mules which she did with surprising ease. They knew, that the most dangerous and unpredictable player was an assassin named Lata who needed to be stopped. The local made gun hanging from the belt on her waist contrasted oddly with her demure looking saree, but Tatya knew better. The plan was to send an empty dingy to the ship… but the army of henchmen and the lunatic Lata stood between Madhavan and his achievement.

The second point of infiltration was at the office front and factory itself; so the incriminating evidence used to prepare the mules could be collected. There were also orders to capture Keva Bai, dead or alive. A team had already been dispatched there and one which had had its eyes on the glass factory was to come into action as soon as the second floor door started opening.

Madhavan had no other choice. From the other end of the bank, he could see Lata shepherding the girls roughly into the dingy. The man managing the boat stood mutely looking at the assault as if it was a very normal issue. He had to remove Lata from the equation. He picked up his radio and called Tatya.

"What is your position, Tatya?"

"Ready sir. Just give me the signal. "

"Ok, she will walk towards you in next five minute…"

Lata was flabbergasted. The boss had never acted so erratically before. Hadn't she just asked her to load the mules? And now, what was so important that she wanted her there in the office? She had actually lost her touch. Since a few years things hadn't been as they used to be. Lata beamed… she had been getting pretty signals that she was the one who was going to be given the ropes soon. A multimillion empire… she touched her protruding belly and smiled endearingly. Yes… yes… babu… momma will be so rich!

She left one of the henchmen in charge and walked reluctantly towards the factory office. There was something wrong, her instincts told her. Why were there so many men on the compound? The place had little role for city men. Instinctively she reached for her gun.

Tatya had been watching the time. He had personally asked PI Madhavan permission to deal with Lata. She had fooled him… since the time she had walked into Gaurang's life. He had treated her like his sister, but now, after the turn of events, he had no doubt that the woman was nothing more than a ruthless killer. Five minutes had passed. He had caught a glimpse of Lata walking towards the office but then she had taken a detour….Tatya stiffened. Where did she go? The cold barrel of the pistol on his neck felt surprisingly comforting on the hot day.

"Bhau, what are you and your men doing here?"

"Vaini, what are you and the goons doing here, and why have you held this gun on my neck?"

Tatya turned slowly his arms in the air. He knew her style already. She loved to shoot from four feet point blank. Something about split heads and deformed faces gave her pleasure.

"Bhau, I kept it for self-protection, after Gaurang's death…." She had moved a step back. Tatya saw the unmistakable swell on her stomach, and his doubts that she had staged her own abortion were confirmed. Lata saw him looking at her 20 weeks of pregnancy and took a step further.

"Vaini, it is very hot, come, I will take you home. What do you say? Some of your famous pooran pouli for me?"

Lata laughed demurely and looked around. There was no other police man in sight. She had liked Tatya as on many occasions he had protected her from the animal, Gaurang. But he or, for that matter, no one was worth enough to give away the gold mine and the bright future. Tatya's presence in the factory right on the day of the shipment was no coincidence. He was here to catch her. He did not have the guts to kill. But she did. And there was no way Tatya was walking away from her. She moved a step back more.

"Oh Bhau, after his death, I stopped going to the house…."

The four bullets hit her heart with such force and accuracy that she couldn't even finish her sentence. Tatya, his service pistol fired for the first time was hot. He walked over to the fallen assassin, the red spot on her chest growing bigger by the second, her eyes open in wonder, and her finger on the trigger of her gun. He decided not to look at the wriggling in her stomach which he knew would stop in a minute. For all practical purposes, she had already told him that her child had died.

CHAPTER THIRTY-SEVEN

A Final Twist

The dingy was full. Revathi had held Charu and directed her to the boat man. Charu recognized him as one of the villagers. On a little afterthought she realized that it was Ratan. Revathi encouraged her to sit close to Ratan as he maneuvered the boat deeper into the sea. Along with the mules, there were two workers in the boat to oversee the on goings. Nature was on their side and the waters were deep and sharp.

Ratan turned the boat to the city. The workers objected sharply and asked him to turn the dingy to the main sea. Ratan pretended not to understand, and continued rowing in the wrong direction. When the angry women came to take matters in their own hands, Revathi clicked handcuffs to them and restrained them both. The girls, drugged but now a little alert were surprised at the turn of events.

The dingy was directed to land and a waiting ambulance took all the mules to the PHC where after a detailed description, name and age of each woman, the pellets were carefully removed by the nurse and Dr. Sagar in presence of a female constable. Those gravely injured were referred, and the mildly hurt ones were treated in the PHC. The total number of pellets, the amount of cocaine, was registered and PI Madhavan was informed. All he could do was whistle in the radio.

****

The remaining workers had seen Lata being shot down. With their captain down, the rest of the workers decided to flee. They were intercepted just outside the factory and taken into custody.

A pair of eyes was looking through thin framed glasses the whole scene. The empire, she had seen being built for last decades was on its last rickety leg, and that too was going to buckle soon. She touched the diamond studs and rearranged her crisp white cotton. Her hair, tied in a bun with a brush of white, was gleaming in the afternoon sun. She wanted to be perfect when they zeroed on her… it was crucial that she should look perfect… she opened the drawer and pulled out a gun. Long back she had learnt how to use it.

****

PI Madhavan wanted to get the boss himself. The prospects of wearing a medal were alluring as they always were to any youngster. He had received the info that Keva Bai was in her office and had made no effort of fleeing. With two other officers he decided to walk in her office and demand surrender. If she resisted, and they hoped she would, they would do the needful.

Everything in the compound was as it was, except the corpses of the henchmen and Lata who were taken down cleverly and tactically. The atmosphere was eerily silent. The officers entered the front door, and the cool interiors and white walls welcomed them. Their leather duty boots made scrunching noises on the polished floors. The office was right in the corner. The sound of the gun shot was muffled. Like the sound made by the fall of a very heavy book. For a moment the officers were not sure whether what they had heard was actually a shot. Instinctively, they ran into the slightly ajar office.

Keva Bai was sitting on the white leather chair, her face blown off leaving her forehead and temples intact. The gun with a silencer lay on her left side. Her saree was in its place, not a thread here or there. Her sandals were still on her feet. Somewhere in the corner of the room her glasses were found. With a little disappointment, PI Madhavan called Dr. Sagar to give him the news, and also to do the needful procedures as the doctor. Madhavan sat in front of his faceless nemesis and tried to fathom what made a human a demon? Maybe there was a demon in all of us and it is important whom we feed.

****

Dr. Sagar examined the corpse with as much detachment as he did the other autopsies. He noticed the gun lying on the left side and spent a minute too much examining the fingers and feet of the dead woman. Then he wrote a report of the cause of dead and requested a full autopsy and left. Madhavan was getting deflated by every passing minute.

****

Revathi was aghast. Sagar's demands had become more and more erratic. She did not understand. Keva Bai was dead. He had married Charu and they were happy and yet, he wanted her to dig out useless and difficult information. About six months back he had asked her to take into account each and every one who was there in the factory on that day and whether everyone was accountable. The long laborious process came up with a single name, and Revathi had no idea how it was going to help Sagar.

"Good. Revathi, can you find out if she had crossed any borders on that particular day?"

"Why? Why are you interested in an inconsequential person?"

"I'm interested because fingers and cracked heels don't lie. Revathi… they don't lie." And with this enigmatic message he left her again to dive into the sea of information to appease his crazy friend.

****

After a month she called him again. She had news. Now, even she was intrigued.

"Where?"

"Bangladesh."

✳✳✳✳✳✳✳✳✳✳✳✳✳

The nurse Shanti Bapat knew what was bothering her that day at the police station. No one, and that meant even the police, knew that the body fished out with the dead child was that of Ganga. The inspector had correctly said that all the bodies were anonymous. But one person knew it and had repeated the fact several times maybe absentmindedly. Since the doctor had paid a visit at her house, she had often wondered what were the doctor's reasons to throw himself in this grime body and soul. And soon, the first day he mentioned that the body was Ganga's, she knew why.

She would not have read the small article at the end of the page, had it not mentioned the doctor by his name. Recently, the nurse had been surprised by the doctor's unusual choice of place of a late honeymoon with Charu. Bangladesh was hardly any girl's dream. And yet there they were. The news heading read:

"Old woman found dead with fingers chopped, in the terrain by newly married Indian couple. Husband being doctor, assumes foul play and passion killing".

✳✳✳✳✳✳✳✳✳✳✳✳✳

"Are you angry Charu? Do you hate me?"

"You need to do a lot more for me to hate you Doctor." Charu snuggled up to Sagar. Last night was a night of disclosures. How Ganga, with a pseudo-identity, had often visited his clinics for abortions had seduced him and made him believe that she loved him. How, she carried his child till almost term and was killed by her own mother... Sagar knew, the moment he saw the toe rings and the child that it was her and his heart had broken although he knew she did not love him...

but for the child who looked so serene and fully developed as if sleeping…and could have been his own son. He had told Charu how he had seen the assumed dead body of Keva Bai but her cracked fingers and heels had given away her identity. He had promised to track the killer of his child, and he did.

Charu snuggled closer and smoothly climbed atop her husband. Her bare breasts and opulent hips stranded over his could feel his manhood slowly responding to her softness and sensuality. Charu knew what the doctor had told her and lots more that no one had ever spoken about or ever would, but they did not matter. What mattered was the look of sorrow and pain in Sagar's eyes being replaced by that of want and desire. Charu bent closer to take charge of her man… for as far as they were concerned, the stories had all ended and were buried.

THE END